How to Write Bestselling Erotica & Erotic Romance

Secrets to Writing Bestselling Tales of Desire

Just Bae

Contents

Introduction

Welcome to the exhilarating journey into erotica and erotica romance writing—a realm where the exploration of desire, intimacy, and passion is woven into the fabric of story-telling. As you embark on this path, your goal extends beyond mere writing. You're aiming to captivate, arouse, and profoundly connect with your readers through narra-tives that resonate with the complexities of human relation-ships and sexuality.

The genres of erotica and erotica romance offer a unique space for writers to delve into the depths of desire, explore the intricacies of human connection, and celebrate the myriad forms of love and expression. Whether your interest lies in the boundary-pushing realms of erotica or the emotionally rich landscapes of erotica romance, you are about to navigate a writing journey that holds the power to move, entertain, and provoke thought.

This book is designed to guide you through crafting stories that not only sizzle on the page but also leave a lasting impression on your readers. From conjuring compelling story ideas that ensnare your audience from the first line to creating dynamic characters whose desires and dilemmas mirror real-world complexities, you'll uncover the essential elements of writing erotica and erotica romance that readers eagerly devour.

Yet, this exploration goes beyond mastering narrative techniques. It's about understanding the pulse of the market, recognizing what readers crave, and learning how to position your stories to reach the enthusiasts who seek them. Whether you envision your work lighting up the screens of e-readers or being whispered about in eager anticipation, the road to success is built upon a deep appreciation of the genre and a strategic approach to engaging with your audience.

We'll dive into the art of crafting erotic scenes that titillate and mesmerize, striking a delicate balance between explicit content and the emotional depth that elevates a story from mere titillation to an unforgettable experience. Discover how to pace your narrative, build tension, and employ language that enlivens the senses, creating immersive scenes that readers can't resist.

Navigating the self-publishing landscape will also be a significant focus, offering you the freedom to bring your stories directly to your readers. From designing captivating covers that draw the eye to employing marketing strategies that build your author brand, you'll learn how to make your mark in the digital world, ensuring your stories find their way into the hands of those who will treasure them.

But at its heart, this book celebrates the transformative power of erotica and erotica romance to explore the full spectrum of human emotion and sexuality. It's a testament to the genre's capacity to open minds, challenge societal norms, and offer readers solace, joy, and arousal.

As we embark on this journey together, keep in mind that the realm of erotica and erotica romance writing is as diverse as the desires it portrays. This rich tapestry has a place for your unique voice and stories. So, let's begin this adventure, ready to create stories that ignite the imagination and awaken the senses. Welcome to the world of erotica and erotica romance writing.

Understanding the desires of erotica and erotica romance readers is crucial for authors navigating these genres, primarily because these readers are seeking more than just a story—they're pursuing an experience. Erotica and erotic romance cater to a spectrum of human emotions and experiences, offering readers a unique blend of fantasy, emotional fulfillment, and, sometimes, a space for exploring their desires and boundaries. The reasons why individuals turn to these genres are as diverse as the readers themselves, highlighting the importance for writers to comprehend these motivations to craft stories that resonate deeply and personally.

Firstly, many readers seek escapism. In a world brimming with routine and responsibilities, erotica and erotic romance offer an escape to worlds where passion, romance, and desire take center stage. These genres provide a sanctuary where readers can indulge in fantasies that might be impractical, unattainable, or even taboo in their everyday lives. By understanding this desire for escapism, authors can create immersive narratives that offer the compelling diversion readers crave.

Another critical aspect is the exploration of desire and sexuality. Erotica and erotic romance serve as a safe space for readers to explore their sexualities and desires without judgment. This exploration can be particularly empowering for readers, offering them a form of validation and the freedom to explore aspects of their identities that they might feel the need to suppress in other areas of their lives. Authors who grasp this aspect can write stories that entertain, affirm, and empower their readers.

Emotional connection and the exploration of relationships also draw readers to these genres. Unlike mainstream romance, where emotional development and relationship dynamics are often the focus, erotica and erotic romance can delve deeper into the complexities of intimacy, power dynamics, and emotional growth. Readers might be looking for stories reflecting their experiences, challenges, and triumphs in relationships. Authors who understand and depict these intricate dynamics can create more meaningful and impactful stories.

Furthermore, the community aspect cannot be overlooked. Readers of erotica and erotic romance often form communities where they can share recommendations, discuss their favorite themes or scenes, and find camaraderie with others who share their interests. This sense of belonging is significant, as it breaks the isolation that can come from societal taboos surrounding sexuality. Authors who engage with these communities gain valuable insights into what readers are actively seeking, enabling them to tailor their writing to meet these expectations.

The desire for high-quality writing and storytelling in erotica and erotic romance is a critical consideration. Readers are not just looking for explicit content; they want well-crafted stories with developed characters, engaging plots, and emotional depth. The misconception that erotica is solely about sexual content underestimates the genre's readers, who appreciate the artistry and skill involved in blending erotic elements with compelling narratives.

An erotica story, at its core, is designed to evoke a visceral response, blending narrative and sexual fantasy to engage readers on a deeply personal level. The structure of such a story often mirrors traditional storytelling but with a distinctive emphasis on the development of sexual tension and intimacy between characters. The main objectives include providing escapism, exploring themes of desire and consent, and delivering a satisfying emotional and physical connection, all while ensuring a coherent and engaging plot.

The foundation of an erotica story typically begins with character introduction, where readers are given a glimpse into the protagonists' lives, desires, and potential conflicts. This stage establishes empathy and interest, drawing readers into the narrative by highlighting relatable or intriguing traits. Characters in erotica are often crafted with a focus on their sexual journey, but grounding them in reality with flaws, ambitions, and personal growth arcs ensures a multi-dimensional appeal.

Following the setup, the narrative moves into the development of sexual tension. This phase is characterized by interactions that hint at or openly express the characters' attraction, desires, and boundaries. The dance of seduction and consent plays a pivotal role here, as it sets the stage for the sexual encounters that are central to the genre. Crafting this tension requires a delicate balance, ensuring it builds gradually and believably towards the story's pivotal moments.

The climax of an erotica story, often a literal and figurative culmination of the built-up sexual tension, serves as a turning point. It's where the characters' emotional vulnerabilities are laid bare, intertwined with their physical intimacy. This is the moment where the narrative delivers on the promise of erotic release. Still, it's also where the emotional stakes are highest, offering a moment of transformation or realization for the characters involved.

Post-climax, the story transitions into resolution, exploring the aftermath of the characters' intimate encounters. This stage involves weaving the sexual experiences into the broader narrative, showing how they have altered the characters' relationships, self-perceptions, or circumstances. It's an opportunity to solidify the emotional bonds formed, resolve any lingering conflicts, and provide closure to the narrative arc.

Throughout these stages, the objective remains to craft scenes of intimacy that resonate with authenticity and emotion. Erotica thrives on the readers' ability to see themselves within the story, to feel the passion, the hesitation, the rush of adrenaline, and the warmth of affection the characters experience. Achieving this requires a keen understanding of human sexuality and the diverse spectrum of desire, ensuring that the story respects and celebrates sexual autonomy and consent.

Moreover, erotica stories often aim to challenge societal norms and explore taboo themes, offering readers a space to question and redefine their boundaries and beliefs about sexuality. This objective underscores the genre's potential for empowerment and liberation, providing a narrative that entertains, enlightens, and provokes thought.

The structure and objectives of an erotica story intertwine to create a narrative that is at once arousing, emotionally engaging, and thought-provoking. By navigating the delicate interplay between desire and emotion, erotica stories invite readers into worlds where the exploration of sexuality is a pathway to personal discovery and transformation. This is where you come in to deliver the goods.

Chapter 1

Difference of Erotica & Erotic Romance

Erotica and Erotic Romance are genres that both delve into the realm of sexual content, yet they cater to different reader expectations and narrative structures. The distinction between the two often hinges on the role that sex and the emotional relationship between characters play within the story. Understanding these fine details is crucial for readers seeking their preferred reading experience and writers aiming to cater to specific audience preferences.

Erotica focuses primarily on the sexual journey of the characters. It is a genre that explores human sexuality with fewer constraints on the narrative's direction, often prioritizing the physical aspects of relationships over emotional development. The main objective of erotica is to evoke a sexual response in the reader, with the narrative structured around sexual encounters and the exploration of sexual fantasies. Characters may experience personal growth or emotional connections, but these are not the story's central focus. Instead, the emphasis is on the characters' sexual experiences and how these experiences drive the plot. An example of this genre is Delta of Venus by Anaïs Nin, a collection of short stories exploring various aspects of sexuality and desire, focusing on the physical and often leaving the emotional as secondary or even tertiary.

Erotic romance, on the other hand, blends the development of a romantic relationship with explicit sexual content. The defining characteristic of this genre is that the romantic relationship is central to the narrative, and the story usually follows the traditional romance arc that ends with a happily ever after (HEA) or happily for now (HFN). In erotic romance, sexual content serves to deepen the emotional connection between the characters, acting as a catalyst for their romantic development. The emotional journey and the establishment of love between the characters are as important, if not more so, than the sexual aspects of their relationship. A classic example of erotic romance is *Fifty Shades of Grey* by E.L. James, which, despite its focus on BDSM and sexual exploration, is structured around the evolving romantic relationship between Anastasia Steele and Christian Grey, leading to a definitive emotional commitment.

The distinction also lies in the reader's journey through the book. Erotica often offers a more exploratory approach to sexuality, potentially without a clear-cut narrative or emotional resolution. It allows readers to delve into fantasies and experiences outside the norm, challenging societal taboos and personal boundaries. This genre can be liberating for readers, offering a spectrum of sexual experiences that emphasize individual desire and exploration over collective norms.

Erotic romance, by providing an emotionally satisfying narrative closure, caters to readers who seek both steamy scenes and emotional depth. The journey through an erotic romance involves not just the thrill of sexual discovery but also the comfort of emotional security and romantic fulfillment. This genre reassures readers that no matter how unconventional the sexual exploration might be, the protagonists will find love and acceptance in each other.

Furthermore, the portrayal of characters differs between the two genres. In erotica, characters may remain more enigmatic or less developed outside of their sexual desires and encounters. This approach allows the reader to project their own fantasies and desires onto the characters, making the sexual exploration more immersive and personal. Erotic romance, however, requires well-rounded characters whose motivations, vulnerabilities, and growth are integral to the story. Their sexual interactions are interwoven with emotional revelations, contributing to the depth of their romantic connection.

The audience for each genre also varies, with some readers preferring the explicit, unfettered exploration of sexuality found in erotica. In contrast, others seek the combination of sexual and emotional fulfillment offered by erotic romance. This distinction is crucial for authors to understand, as it affects everything from the story's pacing and development to the book's marketing and branding.

In terms of narrative structure, erotica may not follow the traditional arc of conflict, climax, and resolution in the same way that erotic romance does. While the conventions of the romance genre bind erotic romance to provide a satisfactory emotional conclusion, erotica has the freedom to explore a more open-ended or unconventional narrative, sometimes leaving conflicts unresolved or the characters' future ambiguous.

This freedom within erotica allows authors to experiment with narrative form, storytelling techniques, and thematic exploration in ways that can push the boundaries of traditional narratives. For instance, erotica may delve into darker themes or more complex psychological territories, exploring the depths of human desire without the necessity of a conventional romantic resolution. This exploration can give readers a more subtle, perhaps even challenging, perspective on sexuality and relationships, reflecting the complexity of human desire, interaction, and often messy realities. Such narratives invite readers to question and contemplate their boundaries regarding human sexuality.

Moreover, the open-mindedness characteristic of erotica does not merely serve as a narrative technique but also as a means to reflect the real-life complexities of sexual and emotional relationships. By not always insisting on a resolution or a clear path forward for the characters, erotica mirrors the ambiguity and ongoing nature of real human experiences. This can offer a form of validation for readers, acknowledging the validity of their experiences that might not fit neatly into the categories of traditional romance or happily-ever-after endings.

Erotica's narrative flexibility also extends to the exploration of identity and self-discovery. Many stories in this genre use sexual experiences as a conduit for character development and self-realization. Without the constraint of aiming for a romantic conclusion, characters in erotica can embark on journeys of self-exploration that prioritize personal growth over romantic attachment. This can be particularly empowering in stories that focus on characters discovering or embracing their sexual orientation, gender identity, or sexual preferences.

The genre's willingness to embrace a variety of sexual expressions and fantasies provides a platform for inclusivity and representation. Erotica can explore the full spectrum of human sexuality, offering stories that resonate with a diverse audience, including those whose desires might be marginalized or underrepresented in mainstream media.

This inclusivity broadens the genre's appeal and is crucial in normalizing and celebrating sexual diversity.

Additionally, the ambiguity and open-ended nature of erotica can serve as a powerful tool for engaging readers' imaginations. By leaving certain aspects of the narrative unresolved or open to interpretation, authors invite readers to become active participants in the story. This engagement can heighten the personal connection to the narrative, allowing readers to fill in the gaps with their own interpretations, desires, and fantasies, making the reading experience uniquely personal and deeply immersive.

In contrast, erotic romance's adherence to the romance genre's conventions does not necessarily limit its scope but instead focuses its narrative lens. By ensuring a satisfying emotional conclusion, erotic romance provides a sense of closure and fulfillment that many readers crave. This structure supports a narrative arc where sexual exploration and emotional development are intertwined, leading to a conclusion that affirms the power of love and emotional connection. While different in their approach and objectives, both erotica and erotic romance offer valuable and distinct experiences to their readers, reflecting the broad and varied landscape of human sexuality and emotional connection.

Chapter 2

Knowing the Market

Knowing the market for erotica and erotic romance is essential for authors looking to connect with their audience and achieve success. The genres have evolved significantly, influenced by cultural shifts, technological advancements, and changing reader preferences. Current trends, reader demographics, and sales insights offer valuable guidance for writers aiming to craft stories that resonate and sell.

One of the prevailing trends in erotica is the exploration of diverse and inclusive narratives. Readers are increasingly seeking stories that represent a wide range of sexual orientations, identities, and relationship dynamics. Books like *The Kiss Quotient* by Helen Hoang, featuring neurodiverse characters and exploring the dynamics of a relationship that defies conventional norms, have found a passionate audience. This shift towards inclusivity reflects a broader societal movement towards acceptance and understanding and opens up new storytelling possibilities for authors.

In erotica romance, the trend of strong, complex female protagonists continues to grow. Readers are looking for characters who are not just objects of desire but active agents in their romantic and sexual journeys. *Bared to You* by Sylvia Day is an example of erotica romance that features a strong, emotionally complex heroine navigating the challenges of a deeply passionate relationship. This trend underscores the shift in reader expectations from passive to empowered female characters.

Another significant trend is the resurgence of specific subgenres, such as historical erotica and erotica romance. The allure of different historical periods, with their unique social dynamics and constraints, offers a fertile ground for exploring sexual and romantic tension. *Pride and Pleasure* by Sylvia Day showcases this trend, combining rich historical detail with steamy erotic scenes, illustrating how the past can be reimagined through the lens of desire.

The rise of self-publishing has also dramatically impacted the erotica and erotica romance markets. Platforms like Amazon's Kindle Direct Publishing have made it easier for authors to reach their audience directly. This democratization of publishing has led to a surge in erotica and erotica romance titles, with works like *Power Play* by Rachel Haimowitz and Cat Grant demonstrating the potential for self-published authors to find success and cultivate a dedicated readership.

Erotica and erotica romance readers are diverse, spanning various age groups, genders, and backgrounds. However, market research suggests a significant portion of the readership is female, aged between 18 and 44. This demographic is not just looking for erotic content but also emotional depth and character-driven stories, indicating a preference for erotic romance that delivers both heat and heart.

Serialized storytelling is another trend gaining traction in the erotica and erotica romance markets. Platforms like Radish offer serialized erotic stories, allowing readers to consume content in bite-sized chunks. This model caters to the modern reader's preference for accessible, engaging content that fits into their busy lives. *The Arrangement* by H.M. Ward is an example of a successful serialized erotica romance, highlighting the potential of episodic storytelling to build an engaged and loyal audience.

The popularity of dark romance and erotica is on the rise, featuring themes of captivity, power play, and taboo relationships. These stories often push the boundaries of traditional romance, exploring the darker aspects of desire and obsession. *Twist Me* by Anna Zaires captures this trend, weaving together intense erotic scenes with a compelling dark narrative, appealing to readers drawn to more edgy and provocative content.

Erotica and erotica romance also increasingly blend with other genres, such as mystery, fantasy, and science fiction. This crossover appeal creates unique narratives that offer both erotic excitement and genre-specific adventures. *The Siren* by Tiffany Reisz, which integrates mystery elements with erotica romance, exemplifies how blending genres can attract readers from different literary preferences, broadening an author's potential market.

Understanding reader preferences and market trends is crucial for erotica and erotica romance authors. Successful writers in these genres stay informed about what readers are looking for, adapting their storytelling to meet those desires while pushing creative boundaries. Engaging with the community through social media, reader forums, and feedback can provide invaluable insights into current trends and demographics, helping authors tailor their work to the market's evolving tastes.

In summary, erotica and erotic romance markets are dynamic, influenced by broader cultural trends, technological advancements, and changing reader expectations. By staying attuned to these shifts and understanding the diverse preferences of their audience, writers can craft compelling, relevant stories that captivate readers and stand out in a competitive marketplace.

Chapter 3

History of Erotica

The history of erotica is as old as literature itself, tracing back to ancient civilizations where the expression of sexual desire and experiences was often interwoven with mythology, poetry, and art. One of the earliest examples of erotic literature is *Kama Sutra,* an ancient Indian text written in Sanskrit by Vātsyāyana. Comprising not just a guide to sexual positions but also advice on love and living a gracious life, *Kama Sutra* reflects the integral role sexuality played in ancient societies' views on harmony and human relationships.

Ancient Greece

In ancient Greece, works like *Lysistrata* by Aristophanes used humor and sexual themes to comment on society and politics. This play, in which women withhold sex from their husbands to end a war, highlights how erotica has long been used not just for arousal but as a tool for social commentary. Similarly, the Roman poet Ovid's *Ars Amatoria ("The Art of Love")* served as a guide to love and seduction in the 1st century BCE, showcasing the longstanding human fascination with the complexities of romantic relationships and sexual attraction.

One of the most iconic works of ancient Greek literature that delves into the erotic is the *Poetry of Sappho*. Hailing from the island of Lesbos, Sappho's lyrical poetry, though only surviving in fragments, vividly expresses the passions and yearnings between women, offering a rare glimpse into female homoerotic desires in antiquity. Her work was so influential that the term "lesbian" is derived from the name of her homeland, emphasizing her impact on the understanding and expression of female sexuality.

The Greeks also celebrated erotic love through their visual arts, with vases, sculptures, and frescoes often depicting sexual acts in a celebratory, sometimes humorous, manner. The explicit pottery from ancient Athens, for example, depicts a range of sexual activities that challenge modern perceptions of ancient societies as prudish or conservative about sex. These artifacts, alongside the myths of gods like Zeus and Aphrodite, who engaged in numerous sexual exploits, underscore the integral role that sexuality played in Greek culture and religion.

Plays and philosophical works of the period frequently explored themes of love and desire. *Plato's Symposium*, a philosophical text presented as a series of speeches at a banquet, discusses the nature of love and beauty, introducing concepts such as Platonic love while acknowledging the beauty of physical attraction and sexual desire. This blend of the intellectual and the sensual in Greek literature and thought highlights the civilization's sophisticated understanding of the many dimensions of sexuality. Through their art, mythology, and philosophy, the ancient Greeks laid the groundwork for Western attitudes toward erotica, celebrating the complexity and beauty of human sexuality in ways that continue to resonate and influence modern erotic literature.

The Middle Ages

Moving into the Middle Ages, the expression of eroticism in literature became more subdued due to religious and cultural constraints. However, erotic undertones can still be found in the poetry and literature of the time, such as in the works of the Persian poet Rumi, whose spiritual writings often blur the lines between divine love and carnal desire. This period also saw the emergence of courtly love literature, where knights and noble ladies engaged in elaborate, often unfulfilled romantic quests, hinting at the erotic tension beneath the surface of chivalric love.

From the 5th to the late 15th century, the Middle Ages often evoke images of a time dominated by religious orthodoxy and strict moral codes, especially concerning sexuality. However, beneath the surface of medieval society's purported chastity, a rich tapestry of erotic literature and art flourished, albeit more subtly and often cloaked in allegory to evade the scrutiny of the Church. This period witnessed the emergence of texts and poetic forms that, while not explicit in the modern sense of erotica, nonetheless engaged with themes of desire, love, and the sensual aspects of human nature.

One of the most significant contributions to erotic literature during the Middle Ages came from the Arabic world, mainly through the collection of stories known as *The Arabian Nights or One Thousand and One Nights*. These tales, compiled over centuries and originating from various cultures, included stories of love, lust, and adventure that celebrated the sensuality and complexity of human relationships. The explicit descriptions of desire and sexual encounters in some of these stories stood in contrast to the more restrained European literature of the time, showcasing the diverse attitudes towards erotica in different parts of the medieval world.

In Europe, the tradition of courtly love presented a unique form of medieval erotica. Though highly idealized and often focusing on unrequited or unconsummated desire, the poetry and literature of courtly love celebrated the emotional and physical longing between knights and noble ladies. Works such as *The Romance of the Rose,* an allegorical French poem, explored the art of seduction and love, veiling its erotic elements within a complex narrative structure that appealed to the nobility's taste for chivalry and romance. This tradition underscored the period's capacity for subtlety in erotic expression, embedding sensual themes within socially acceptable narratives.

The Middle Ages also saw the creation of fabliaux, short comic tales written in verse that were popular in France. Unlike the lofty ideals of courtly love, fabliaux were earthy, crude, and often sexually explicit, poking fun at all levels of society, including the clergy. These stories, with their irreverent humor and candid exploration of sexual themes, provided a counterpoint to the more sanitized official culture, revealing a public appetite for ribald and erotic content. The fabliaux's frankness about bodily functions and sexual exploits offered a glimpse into the everyday people's attitudes towards sexuality, challenging the notion of the Middle Ages as an era of universal prudishness.

Furthermore, the medieval period was a time of significant religious and philosophical writings that, paradoxically, contributed to its erotic literature. Theologians and philosophers wrote extensively about the nature of love, often drawing a line between carnal desire and spiritual love. However, in works like The Decameron by Giovanni Boccaccio, written in the wake of the Black Death, the narratives are filled with sexual exploits and adventures, reflecting a society that, while outwardly pious, was deeply fascinated by the pleasures and complexities of earthly love. This duality of medieval thought provided a rich ground for the exploration of erotic themes, bridging the gap between the sacred and the profane.

The Renaissance

The Renaissance reignited interest in human sexuality with works like The Decameron by Giovanni Boccaccio, a collection of novellas that includes tales of love, lust, and deception. This period celebrated the human form and experience, leading to more explicit explorations of sexual themes in literature. It was a period of rebirth in art, literature, and culture across Europe, marking a significant shift in the portrayal and acceptance of erotic themes in literature. From the 14th to the 17th century, this era witnessed a resurgence of interest in humanism, the classics, and an exploration of human sexuality that was more openly accepted than the often-repressive Middle Ages. The revival of classical texts, coupled with a burgeoning sense of individualism and a more secular outlook, provided fertile ground for the exploration of erotic themes.

One of the seminal works of the period is Giovanni Boccaccio's *The Decameron,* which was composed in the 14th century. This collection of novellas, set against the backdrop of the Black Death in Florence, is notable for its candid and often humorous portrayal of sexual adventures and misadventures. Boccaccio's work reflects the human condition in its myriad forms, including the pursuit of love and sexual gratification, making it a cornerstone of Renaissance literature that challenged its time's moral and social conventions.

The Renaissance also saw the re-publication of Ovid's Ars *Amatoria (The Art of Love)* in many European languages, reigniting interest in this classical work that served as both a love guide and a repository of seduction techniques. The widespread interest in Ovid's work during the Renaissance underscores the period's fascination with love, desire, and the strategies employed in pursuing sexual relationships. This period laid the groundwork for a finer understanding of the complexities of love and sexuality, with artists and writers drawing inspiration from ancient myths and texts to explore these themes in their works.

In art, the Renaissance's exploration of erotic themes was not limited to literature. The era is renowned for its advancements in visual arts, with artists like Titian and Michelangelo pushing the boundaries of how the nude body and sensual themes were portrayed. Titian's Venus of Urbino and Michelangelo's sculptures and paintings celebrated the human form in its naked beauty, embodying the Renaissance's embrace of sensuality and the erotic. These works, while not explicit in the modern sense, conveyed a deep appreciation for physical beauty and desire, influencing the perception of eroticism in art and society.

Furthermore, the Renaissance contributed to the development of the sonnet, a poetic form that often explored themes of love and desire. Poets like Petrarch and Shakespeare crafted sonnets that delved into the complexities of love, longing, and the beloved's beauty, elevating personal feelings of desire to high art. With their intricate form and emotional depth, these sonnets exemplify the Renaissance's contribution to erotic literature, blending the intellectual with the sensual in ways that celebrate the full spectrum of human love and desire.

The Renaissance period, with its focus on humanism, the revival of classical antiquity, and the flourishing of arts and literature, significantly shaped the evolution of erotica. By integrating the sensual with the intellectual and the spiritual, the Renaissance laid the groundwork for a richer, more complex understanding of eroticism that would continue to evolve in the centuries to follow.

The 18th Century

The 18th century marked a significant era in the development of erotica, characterized by a mix of burgeoning Enlightenment ideals, increasing literacy rates, and a covert fascination with the sensual and the sexual. This period saw the publication of some of the most notorious and enduring works of erotic literature, reflecting both the refinement and the ribaldry of the age. The era's erotica often navigated the tension between public morality and private desire, offering insights into the complex sexual politics of the time.

One of the most iconic works of 18th-century erotica is *Fanny Hill,* or *Memoirs of a Woman of Pleasure* by John Cleland, first published in 1748. Written while Cleland was in debtor's prison, Fanny Hill is considered the first original English prose pornography. The novel recounts the life of its titular character, detailing her journey from innocence to sexual awakening and her subsequent adventures in the world of pleasure. Despite—or perhaps because of—its explicit content, *Fanny Hill* faced legal challenges and bans. Yet, it has endured as a seminal work in the canon of erotic literature, notable for its vivid depiction of sexual encounters and its exploration of desire and economic survival.

The Marquis de Sade, though more closely associated with the late 18th and early 19th centuries, significantly influenced the genre with his libertine novels. Works such as *Justine and Juliette* pushed the boundaries of erotic literature, intertwining narratives of sex and violence in a way that scandalized and fascinated readers. De Sade's writings, filled with philosophical musings on freedom, nature, and societal norms, challenged conventional morality and introduced themes of sadism (a term derived from his name), making him a controversial figure whose works were banned for much of history.

Another pivotal era figure was Giacomo Casanova, known for his autobiography, The *Story of My Life*, which detailed his European exploits and adventures. Casanova's memoirs, rich with tales of seduction and escapades, offer a glimpse into the libertine lifestyle of the time and have cemented his legacy as history's quintessential seducer. His accounts, though not purely erotica, are imbued with erotic undertones that capture the spirit of 18th-century sexual adventurism.

The 18th century also witnessed the rise of erotic prints and illustrations, which accompanied many texts of the period. Artists like Thomas Rowlandson and William Hogarth produced works that, while often satirical, did not shy away from depicting the bawdy aspects of life. These illustrations were integral to the era's erotic literature, providing visual accompaniment to the scandalous tales and contributing to the reader's overall experience.

In France, *Les Liaisons Dangereuses* by Choderlos de Laclos, published in 1782, offered a whiffed portrayal of seduction, manipulation, and the moral complexities of the aristocracy. The novel's exploration of sexual politics through the epistolary format was innovative and incendiary, making it one of the era's most provocative works. Its enduring popularity underscores the fascination with narratives that reveal the darker aspects of human nature and desire.

Erotic literature in the 18th century was not solely the province of the elite; it also found an audience among the burgeoning middle class. The proliferation of print culture and the rise of the novel as a popular literary form made erotic works more accessible. Books like The *School of Venus* or *The Ladies Delight*, though less known today, were widely read at the time, catering to the public's appetite for sexual education disguised as entertainment.

This period also saw the emergence of female voices in erotica, though often anonymized or pseudonymous due to the social risks involved. The novel *Memoirs of a Woman of Pleasure* is one such example, offering perspectives on female desire and agency within the constraints of the era's gender norms. These works not only provided titillation but also subtly challenged the patriarchal structures that sought to control female sexuality.

The 18th century's contributions to the field of erotica set the stage for the more explicit explorations of sexuality that would emerge in the following centuries. By intertwining the intellectual with the sensual, the period's writers and artists laid the groundwork for a literary tradition that continues to probe the depths of human desire. The era's erotica, with its blend of scandal, satire, and sensuality, remains a fascinating study in the evolution of sexual expression, reflecting the social, cultural, and philosophical currents of the time.

The Victorian Era

The Victorian era, spanning from 1837 to 1901 under the reign of Queen Victoria, is often characterized by its strict moral codes and prudish attitudes towards sex. However, beneath this veneer of respectability thrived a robust under-current of erotic literature and art, revealing a complex relationship between the Victorians and sexuality. This period was marked by a paradoxical blend of repression and exploration, where the public discourse on morality clashed with private desires and curiosities.

One of the most notorious examples of Victorian erotica is *"My Secret Life,"* an anonymous autobiography published in the late 19th century. This extensive work, attributed to a figure known only as "Walter," offers a detailed and unapologetic account of the author's sexual exploits and observations in Victorian society. Its explicit content and candid exploration of prostitution, voyeurism, and various sexual practices challenged the period's outward conservatism, making it a scandalous yet fascinating document of the era's hidden desires.

The publication of *"The Pearl,"* a famous magazine from 1879 to 1880, further illustrates the Victorians' secret fascination with erotica. Filled with bawdy stories, poems, and serial novels, *"The Pearl"* catered to an audience eager for sexual content that was otherwise suppressed in mainstream culture. Its existence, along with other similar publications, underscores the demand for erotic literature that existed in stark contrast to the era's public prudishness.

Victorian erotica also saw the advent of photographic pornography, a development made possible by advances in photographic technology. Though the production and distribution of such material were illegal and carried significant risk, it nonetheless circulated widely in private circles. These early forays into photographic erotica demonstrate the era's technological ingenuity as well as its persistent interest in exploring sexuality through new mediums.

Erotic literature of the Victorian era often employed euphemisms and allegorical tales to veil its explicit content, navigating the tightrope of moral acceptability while still catering to its audience's desires. Works like *"Venus in Furs"* by Leopold von Sacher-Masoch explored themes of masochism and power dynamics, influencing the discourse on sexuality in subtle yet profound ways. Sacher-Masoch's depiction of a man's desire to be dominated by a woman challenged traditional gender roles and introduced the term "masochism" to the lexicon of sexual behavior.

The prevalence of "flagellation literature" during this period further reveals the Victorians' fascination with BDSM themes. Books and pamphlets depicting spanking and whipping as forms of punishment or erotic stimulation were surprisingly widespread, suggesting a societal undercurrent that contradicted the era's official stance on sexual propriety.

These works, often framed as moral instruction, provided a socially acceptable guise for the exploration of sado-masochistic desires.

Despite the thriving underground market for erotica, the Victorian era was also a time of intense legal and social efforts to suppress obscene material. The Obscene Publications Act of 1857 was a significant legal measure that sought to eradicate the distribution of pornographic literature, leading to high-profile raids and prosecutions. This legislation highlights the period's complex dynamics of censorship, where the state's attempts to control sexuality only seemed to fuel its clandestine consumption.

Female authors and protagonists began to emerge in Victorian erotica, challenging the male-dominated perspective that characterized much of the genre. While still rare and often published anonymously, works by and about women explored themes of female desire, autonomy, and sexual awakening. These narratives, though constrained by the period's gender norms, offered a counterpoint to the predominantly male gaze of erotic literature, hinting at the beginnings of a more inclusive exploration of sexuality.

The Victorian era's contribution to the evolution of erotica is a testament to the enduring human interest in sexuality despite societal restrictions. The period's erotic literature and art, with their blend of concealment and exploration, reflect a society grappling with the tension between public decency and private desires. As such, Victorian erotica serves as a fascinating study in contrasts, offering insight into the complexities of 19th-century attitudes toward sex and the subversive ways in which people sought to express and fulfill their sexual needs.

The 20th Century

The 20th century heralded profound transformations in erotica, mirroring the era's sweeping societal, cultural, and technological changes. This period witnessed the gradual dismantling of Victorian prudishness, giving way to more open expressions of sexuality in literature and art. As the century progressed, shifts in social attitudes, the advent of feminist and LGBTQ+ movements, and legal battles over censorship collectively reshaped the landscape of erotic expression.

In the early decades, the publication of works like D.H. Lawrence's Lady Chatterley's Lover in 1928 marked a significant moment for erotica. Lawrence's novel, with its explicit descriptions of sexual intercourse and its emphasis on physical and emotional connection, faced widespread bans and censorship. Yet, its eventual legal victories in obscenity trials during the 1950s and 60s in the United States and the United Kingdom were pivotal in challenging legal restrictions on literature, setting a precedent for the freedom of expression and paving the way for future publications of erotic content.

The mid-20th century also saw the rise of the sexual revolution, a movement that significantly influenced the creation and consumption of erotic literature. This era, characterized by a pushback against traditional norms governing sexuality and gender, saw the publication of Fear of Flying by Erica Jong in 1973. Jong's novel, known for its frank and liberating exploration of female sexuality and desire, epitomized the changing attitudes toward women's erotic agency and became a landmark work in feminist literature.

The latter half of the 20th century was marked by the emergence of LGBTQ+ erotica and romance, reflecting broader societal shifts toward the recognition and acceptance of diverse sexual orientations and identities. Works such as Giovanni's Room by James Baldwin, published in 1956, offered subtle insights into homosexual relationships at a time when such topics were often taboo. The growth of LGBTQ+ publishing houses and the increasing visibility of queer stories contributed to a more inclusive understanding of erotic desire, challenging heteronormative assumptions and expanding the genre's scope.

The advent of the internet and digital technology in the late 20th century revolutionized the distribution and accessibility of erotica, allowing for a proliferation of content and the formation of online communities centered around erotic literature and fan fiction. Websites and forums provided platforms for sharing and discussing erotic stories, catering to a wide range of interests and fetishes. This democratization of content creation and consumption enabled writers and readers to explore niche desires and identities, significantly diversifying the landscape of erotica.

Erotica in the 20th century also became a medium for political and social commentary, with writers using erotic narratives to explore issues of power, inequality, and liberation. Anaïs Nin's Delta of Venus, published posthumously in the 1970s but written in the 1940s, is celebrated for its literary quality and exploration of the power dynamics within sexual relationships. Nin's work, along with that of other writers, demonstrated how erotica could transcend mere titillation to engage with deeper philosophical and societal questions.

The genre's evolution was further influenced by landmark legal cases and the establishment of rating systems for books and films, which sought to balance freedom of expression with the protection of public morals. The trials of Lady Chatterley's Lover, Tropic of Cancer by Henry Miller, and other works challenged the legal boundaries of obscenity, leading to a gradual liberalization of publishing laws. These legal battles highlighted the tension between artistic expression and societal standards, a theme that would continue to play out across the century.

As the 20th century drew to a close, the lines between erotica and mainstream literature became increasingly blurred, with erotic themes permeating popular novels and films. The success of series such as The Vampire Chronicles by Anne Rice, which combined elements of horror, romance, and erotica, reflected changing public tastes and the growing acceptance of erotic content in mainstream culture. This trend towards the eroticization of popular media hinted at the evolving nature of erotica, setting the stage for its continued expansion in the 21st century.

The 20th century stands as a pivotal era in the history of erotica, characterized by significant shifts in how erotic content was produced, consumed, and perceived. Through a combination of legal victories, cultural movements, and technological advancements, erotica emerged from the shadows of censorship to claim a more visible and varied presence in the cultural landscape, reflecting the complex, changing nature of human sexuality.

Modern-Day

The modern era has witnessed a remarkable transformation in the landscape of erotica, characterized by its mainstream acceptance, digital revolution, and the diversification of themes and voices. This period has seen erotica emerge from the fringes to become a significant part of popular culture, facilitated by technological advancements, changing societal attitudes towards sexuality, and the influence of pivotal literary works.

The early 2000s saw the internet becoming an essential platform for disseminating and consuming erotica. Online forums, websites, and e-publishing platforms allowed authors to bypass traditional publishing barriers, reaching audiences directly with a wide array of erotic content. This digital revolution democratized erotica, enabling niche and previously underrepresented themes to find a readership. Websites like Literotica and the advent of e-readers contributed to the genre's proliferation, offering anonymity and ease of access that expanded its audience.

One of the most significant milestones in modern erotica was the publication and unprecedented success of *Fifty Shades of Grey* by E.L. James in 2011. Originally conceived as Twilight fan fiction, the series catapulted erotica into the mainstream spotlight, breaking sales records and sparking a global conversation about BDSM and sexual fantasies. The trilogy's impact was manifold; it not only boosted the erotica genre's profile but also led to a surge in the publication of erotic romance, influencing publishers and authors to explore similar themes.

The Fifty Shades phenomenon also had a profound effect on the romance genre, blurring the lines between romance and erotica. The success of these books encouraged more explicit sexual content in mainstream romance novels, leading to the emergence of "erotic romance" as a popular subgenre. This hybrid genre combined the emotional depth and happy endings associated with traditional romance with the open-door approach to sex scenes found in erotica.

An increased focus on diversity and representation in erotica has also characterized the modern era. LGBTQ+ erotica and erotic romance have gained prominence, reflecting and contributing to broader societal movements toward inclusivity. Authors and publishers have become more attuned to the importance of representing a range of sexual orientations, gender identities, and relationship dynamics, offering readers stories that reflect their experiences and fantasies. *Works like Call Me By Your Name* by André Aciman, published in 2007, have been celebrated for their beautiful and shaded exploration of queer love and passion.

Feminist erotica has risen in prominence, challenging traditional power dynamics and emphasizing consent, female pleasure, and agency. This shift is part of a broader feminist movement within society, which seeks to reclaim erotica from the male gaze and create content that empowers women. Collections like *The Sexy Librarian's Big Book of Erotica*, edited by Rose Caraway, showcase the diversity and creativity of feminist erotica, offering stories that cater to a wide range of desires and perspectives.

The modern era has also seen the rise of self-publishing and indie authors in erotica, facilitated by platforms like Amazon's Kindle Direct Publishing. This has allowed for greater experimentation and the exploration of niche interests, from paranormal romance to historical erotica, catering to the specific tastes of diverse readerships. The success of self-published authors has challenged traditional publishing norms and demonstrated the viability of erotica as a literary genre.

Finally, the conversation around erotica in the modern era has evolved to include discussions about the impact of pornography on society and relationships. The easy accessibility of online pornography has sparked debates about its influence on sexual expectations and behaviors, leading some erotica authors to emphasize emotional connectivity and realistic portrayals of sex in their work as a counterpoint. This has led to a detailed dialogue about the distinctions between erotica and pornography, with erotica being celebrated for its ability to explore the psychological and emotional aspects of sexual relationships.

In summary, the modern era of erotica is marked by its mainstream success, digital accessibility, and the broadening of its thematic horizons. As societal attitudes towards sex continue to evolve, erotica remains a dynamic and ever-expanding genre, reflecting the complexities of human desire and the ongoing quest for sexual expression and understanding.

Chapter 4

Influences

The landscape of erotica and erotic romance literature is as diverse and complex as the tapestry of human desire, encompassing a broad spectrum of themes, narratives, and explorations of intimacy. From the pioneering works of Anaïs Nin, which laid the groundwork for the acceptance and appreciation of female sexual agency in literature, to the contemporary tales of BDSM and polyamory that challenge conventional boundaries of love and desire, these genres offer a profound insight into the myriad ways in which sexuality and emotion can intertwine. Works such as *Fifty Shades of Grey* by E.L. James have catapulted these once-niche genres into the mainstream, sparking conversations about sexual freedom, consent, and romantic dynamics. Meanwhile, novels like *The Kiss Quotient* by Helen Hoang and *Call Me by Your Name* by André Aciman broaden the scope of erotic romance by incorporating diverse perspectives and experiences, thereby enriching the genre with tales of neurodiversity and queer love. These narratives not only provide escapism and pleasure but also serve as a mirror reflecting the evolving societal attitudes toward sexuality, relationships, and self-discovery. As we delve into case studies of influential erotica and erotic romance novels, we uncover the transformative power of these stories to both entertain and enlighten, challenging readers to explore the depths of their own desires and the complexities of human connection.

Delta of Venus by Anaïs Nin is a seminal work in the erotica genre, offering a collection of short stories that delve into various aspects of desire and sexuality. Nin's pioneering approach to female sexuality and erotic expression in the mid-20th century was groundbreaking. Her writing style, which combines eloquence with explicitness, has made Delta of Venus a classic, showcasing the potential of erotica to explore the depth and complexity of human desire beyond mere physical acts.

The Story of O by Pauline Réage is another classic that has left a significant mark on the landscape of erotic literature. Published in 1954, it tells the story of a Parisian fashion photographer, O, and her willing submission to her lovers. Its exploration of BDSM and consent pushed the boundaries of what was socially acceptable at the time, inviting readers to reconsider their boundaries and fantasies. The novel's controversial reception and enduring popularity underscore

the intrigue and complexity surrounding themes of dominance and submission.

Call Me by Your Name by André Aciman explores the erotic
awakening and passionate love affair between two young
men, Elio and Oliver, in Italy during the 1980s. Aciman's
exquisite portrayal of longing, desire, and heartbreak transcends the typical boundaries of erotic romance, offering a
poignant exploration of first love and sexual discovery. The
novel's success, bolstered by a critically acclaimed film
adaptation, highlights the universal appeal of stories that
capture the intensity and complexity of human emotion and
connection.

Captivated by You from Sylvia Day's Crossfire series
exemplifies how erotic romance can weave deep emotional
narratives with explicit sexual content. The series chronicles the tumultuous relationship between Eva and Gideon,
both survivors of abuse, exploring themes of healing, trust,
and mutual growth. Day's ability to address these heavy
themes within the framework of a sexually charged
romance speaks to the genre's capacity for depth and
empathy, resonating with readers seeking both heat and
heart.

Dark Lover, the first book in J.R. Ward's Black Dagger
Brotherhood series, combines elements of paranormal
romance with erotica, setting a new standard for the genre.
The novel introduces a secret society of vampire warriors

and their battle against dehumanization, wrapped around the steamy and emotionally charged romance.

Lady Chatterley's Lover by D.H. Lawrence is a pioneering work in the realm of erotic literature, breaking significant ground in depicting the physical and emotional aspects of a sexual relationship. Published in 1928 and subjected to numerous obscenity trials, Lawrence's novel challenges the social norms of its time, advocating for the importance of physical intimacy as a natural and vital component of the human experience. The story of Lady Chatterley and her affair with the gamekeeper, Oliver Mellors, explores themes of class, love, and the disconnect between mind and body in early 20th-century society. Its enduring influence underscores the power of erotica to question societal norms and champion the cause of sexual freedom and expression.

The Sleeping Beauty Quartet by A.N. Roquelaure (a pseudonym of Anne Rice) takes a bold dive into the world of BDSM and consensual power exchange. Starting with The Claiming of Sleeping Beauty, this series reimagines the classic fairy tale as an erotic journey of awakening and submission. Rice's foray into erotica with these novels has been both controversial and influential, pushing the boundaries of the genre with its explicit scenes of domination and submission set within a fantastical narrative. The series has not only captivated readers with its erotic allure but also sparked discussions on the dynamics of power, consent, and desire in literature.

Fear of Flying by Erica Jong is a landmark novel exploring female sexuality, desire, and independence. Published in 1973, it introduces readers to Isadora Wing, who embarks on a journey of self-discovery and sexual liberation. Jong's candid and humorous narrative voice, combined with explicit sexual content, made Fear of Flying a revolutionary work that resonated with the feminist movement and opened the door for more open discussions about women's erotic desires and frustrations.

Lolita by Vladimir Nabokov, while not erotica in the traditional sense, has exerted a significant influence on the genre and the broader literary landscape through its controversial exploration of obsession, desire, and manipulation. The novel's intricate prose and the moral ambiguities of its narrator, Humbert Humbert, challenge readers to confront their reactions to the taboo subject matter. Nabokov's work remains a complex study of the dark corners of human desire, demonstrating the power of erotic themes to provoke thought and controversy.

Tropic of Cancer by Henry Miller, published in 1934, broke new ground with its frank discussion of sex, free from the constraints of decency or morality. Miller's autobiographical novel set in Paris was banned in the United States and the United Kingdom for decades due to its explicit content. Its eventual publication marked a significant moment in the battle for freedom of expression, influencing not just the genre of erotica but the entire literary world by championing the right to explore human sexuality with honesty and without censorship.

Vox by Nicholson Baker is a modern exploration of erotica, focusing on an intimate conversation between two strangers on a phone sex line. Published in 1992, the novel's detailed and explicit dialogue-based exploration of fantasies and desires was groundbreaking. Baker's work is a testament to the power of words to evoke eroticism and intimacy, proving that explicit content can be both intellectually engaging and sensually arousing.

Story of the Eye by Georges Bataille, published in 1928, is a short novel that delves into the surreal and grotesque in its depiction of the sexual escapades of two teenagers. Its exploration of the themes of transgression, desire, and the violation of societal norms has made it a cult classic in erotic literature. Bataille's work challenges readers to reconsider the boundaries between eroticism and horror, pushing the envelope of what can be considered erotic literature.

The End of Alice by A.M. Homes is a controversial novel that explores the dark and taboo aspects of desire through the correspondence between a convicted pedophile and a nineteen-year-old girl. Homes' unflinching examination of forbidden desire and the psychological depth of her characters challenge the reader's comfort zones, making it a provocative addition to the genre. This novel demonstrates how erotica can be used to explore the complexities of human sexuality and the moral dilemmas it often presents.

Crash by J.G. Ballard is a novel that intertwines sexual desire with technology and the macabre, exploring the sexual fetishization of car crashes. Ballard's work is a seminal exploration of how modernity, technology, and eroticism can intersect in disturbing yet fascinating ways. The novel's impact on the genre lies in its ability to push the boundaries of erotic fiction, inviting readers to explore their responses to its unconventional themes.

The Gargoyle by Andrew Davidson, while not strictly an erotica novel, weaves elements of romance, mythology, and historical fiction into a narrative that includes intensely erotic moments. The novel's exploration of love, redemption, and the transformative power of storytelling spans centuries, demonstrating the capacity of erotic and romantic elements to deepen narrative complexity and emotional resonance.

Chapter 5

Genres

Erotica is a genre of literature that focuses on the depiction of sexual relationships and erotic themes. It is designed to arouse and entertain, offering readers a sophisticated exploration of desire, passion, and intimate connections. Unlike pornography, which often prioritizes explicit sexual imagery with the primary intent of sexual arousal, erotica incorporates a narrative and character development, making the sexual content part of a broader, often emotionally rich story. This distinction is crucial in understanding the appeal and purpose of erotica in the literary world.

Contemporary Erotica

Contemporary erotica is set in the present day and reflects modern societal norms and sexual practices. These stories often explore the complexities of current relationships, including the dynamics of online dating, casual sex, and the fluidity of sexual orientation and gender identity. Contemporary erotica resonates with readers looking for sexual exploration and experiences that mirror the complexities of today's world.

Urban Erotica

Set in contemporary urban settings, these stories explore the sexual experiences of characters navigating city life. Themes often include the complexities of modern relationships, the anonymity of city living, and the pursuit of pleasure amidst the chaos. Urban erotica is known for its gritty, realistic portrayal of desire.

Interracial Erotica

Features characters of different racial or ethnic backgrounds, exploring the intersections of culture, race, and desire. These stories can challenge stereotypes and address cultural tensions, all while celebrating the beauty of diversity in erotic encounters. Interracial erotica promotes inclusivity and understanding through the lens of passion.

Historical Erotica

Historical erotica transports readers to bygone eras, blending sexual adventures with the rich tapestry of history. These narratives can be set in any historical period, from ancient civilizations to the recent past, and often incorporate historical accuracy with erotic imagination. The allure of historical erotica lies in its ability to juxtapose the sexual mores of the past with timeless human desires, offering a tantalizing escape into history's sensual secrets.

Paranormal Erotica

Paranormal erotica delves into the supernatural, featuring characters such as vampires, werewolves, ghosts, and other mythical creatures. These stories blend elements of fantasy and horror with eroticism, creating a unique space for exploring unconventional desires and power dynamics. The appeal of paranormal erotica lies in its ability to push the boundaries of the imagination, offering readers an escape into worlds where the erotic intermingles with the uncanny.

BDSM Erotica

BDSM erotica focuses on narratives that explore the dynamics of power, control, and consent within sexual relationships. These stories encompass a range of practices and preferences, including bondage, discipline, dominance, submission, sadism, and masochism. BDSM erotica offers a deep dive into the psychological aspects of power exchange and the eroticism of surrender, providing a safe space for readers to explore these themes.

Romantic Erotica

Romantic erotica blends the emotional depth of romance with the heat of erotic fiction. These stories prioritize the development of romantic relationships alongside sexual exploration, offering narratives where passion and emotional connection are inseparable. Romantic erotica appeals to readers who seek not just the physical but also the emotional dimensions of sexual relationships.

LGBTQ+ Erotica

LGBTQ+ erotica features stories centered around lesbian, gay, bisexual, transgender, queer, and other non-heteronormative identities and relationships. This subgenre provides representation and explores the diverse spectrum of human sexuality and gender identity through erotic narratives. LGBTQ+ erotica is significant for its role in empowering and validating the experiences of LGBTQ+ individuals, offering stories that reflect the richness of their lives and desires.

Fantasy and Sci-Fi Erotica

Fantasy and sci-fi erotica merge the imaginative settings and elements of fantasy and science fiction with erotic themes. These stories can transport readers to fantastical worlds or futuristic societies where sexual norms and relationships may differ vastly from those in the real world. This subgenre offers a playground for exploring desire without limits, where the only boundaries are those of the writer's imagination.

Erotic Suspense and Thrillers

Erotic suspense and thrillers combine elements of mystery, danger, and sexuality. These narratives keep readers on the edge of their seats with plots that involve crimes, secrets, and intense power dynamics, all while incorporating explicit sexual content. The tension between the suspenseful plot and the erotic scenes adds a thrilling layer to the reading experience.

Erotic Poetry

Erotic poetry is a form of erotica that uses poetic techniques to convey themes of desire, love, and sexual experiences. This subgenre allows for a more abstract and lyrical exploration of eroticism, with poets using imagery, metaphor, and rhythm to evoke sensual landscapes and intimate moments. Erotic poetry is celebrated for its ability to capture the essence of human sexuality in an artful manner.

Erotic Horror

Erotic horror combines elements of horror fiction with eroticism, exploring the intersection of fear, death, and desire. These stories might feature themes of vampirism, monsters, or other horror tropes intertwined with sexual content. The fusion of horror and erotica challenges readers to confront the darker aspects of desire and the unknown, offering a uniquely intense reading experience.

Erotic Comedy

Erotic comedy blends humor with erotic content, offering a light-hearted and often playful take on sexual themes. These stories can parody erotic conventions, explore sexual mishaps, or employ comedic timing in sexual encounters, providing entertainment that is both arousing and amusing. Erotic comedy is a reminder of the joy and humor found in human sexuality.

Cyberpunk Erotica

Cyberpunk erotica incorporates the themes and aesthetics of the cyberpunk genre, such as advanced technology, dystopian futures, and cybernetic enhancements, into erotic narratives. These stories explore how technology intersects with human sexuality, offering visions of future sexualities shaped by technological advancement. Cyberpunk erotica invites readers to imagine the possibilities of desire in the digital age, where the lines between human and machine blur.

Menage and Polyamory Romance (can be erotic or not)

Menage and polyamory romance can explore elements of the complexities and joys of relationships involving more than two people. These stories challenge traditional monogamous paradigms, offering insights into the dynamics of polyamorous love, jealousy, and the negotiation of boundaries. Through a focus on communication, consent, and emotional growth, menage and polyamory erotic romance celebrate the diversity of human relationships and the many forms that love can take.

Erotic Suspense

Combining the thrill of suspense with the intensity of erotic romance, this subgenre weaves together danger, mystery, and passion. Characters may find themselves entangled in crimes, secrets, or difficult situations they must navigate together, all while developing a deep, often fraught romantic connection. Erotic suspense romance keeps readers on the edge of their seats, both for the resolution of the suspense and the culmination of the romance.

Medical Erotica

Medical erotica revolves around sexual encounters in medical settings involving doctors, nurses, and patients and the exploration of medical fetishes. This subgenre explores themes of care, authority, and vulnerability associated with medical examinations and treatments, offering a distinct blend of trust, power dynamics, and eroticism.

Erotic Thrillers

Erotic thrillers combine elements of mystery, suspense, and eroticism, creating a tense and titillating narrative experience. These stories often involve crimes of passion, dangerous liaisons, and the intersection of desire and deception. Erotic thrillers keep readers guessing not only about the outcome of the plot but also about the evolving dynamics of the characters' sexual relationships.

Gothic Erotica

Gothic erotica combines the dark, brooding atmospheres of gothic literature with erotic storytelling. This subgenre is characterized by tales of passion and obsession set against the backdrop of ominous castles, haunted landscapes, and forbidden romances. Gothic erotica evokes a sense of mystery and danger, weaving together the threads of horror, romance, and eroticism.

Erotic Adventure

Erotic adventure tales whisk readers away on journeys of danger, exploration, and sexual discovery. These stories often feature protagonists embarking on quests or adventures in exotic locations, where the thrill of the unknown fuels their erotic encounters. This subgenre blends the excitement of adventure fiction with the pleasure of erotic storytelling, offering a dynamic reading experience.

Chapter 6

How to Craft your Erotic Story

Crafting an erotic story is an artful journey into the exploration of desire, intimacy, and the dynamics of human relationships. It requires a delicate balance between evoking the sensual and capturing the emotional, all while weaving a narrative that enthralls and engages the reader's deepest fantasies and feelings. This process goes beyond the mere depiction of sexual encounters; it involves creating complex characters whose desires, fears, and motivations are intricately linked to their sexual experiences. A compelling erotic story invites the reader into a world where the physical and the emotional are inextricably intertwined, offering a space for exploration, discovery, and, sometimes, transformation. Through careful character development, vivid sensory details, and a compelling plot, writers can craft stories that resonate on multiple levels, challenging perceptions and celebrating the diversity of human sexuality. Whether set in the realms of the realistic or the fantastical, crafting an erotic story is about capturing the essence of desire in all its forms, creating a tapestry of narratives that reflect the richness and complexity of the human heart.

Crafting characters is more than just their physical desires; it's about creating personas with depth, conflict, and aspirations that resonate with your readers. Think of *The Sexual Life* of Catherine M. by Catherine Millet, a memoir that delves deep into the personal sexual experiences of its author. Catherine's narrative is compelling because she's not just a participant in various sexual escapades but a fully realized individual with complex thoughts and feelings about her actions. Like Catherine, your characters should have backgrounds and personalities that inform their desires, making their journeys not just about steamy experiences but about personal discovery and transformation.

When building tension and pacing in your erotic scenes, consider how anticipation can be as potent as fulfillment. In *Story of O* by Pauline Réage, the anticipation and psychological aspects of O's experiences are meticulously crafted, creating a palpable tension that engages readers before any explicit action occurs. Your scenes should simmer with this kind of anticipation, using dialogue, setting, and character thoughts to build up to the erotic moments, making the eventual climax all the more satisfying for the reader.

Erotica often allows for a more direct exploration of sexual experiences than erotic romance, focusing on the immediacy of desire and fulfillment. However, even within this framework, pacing can vary. In *Delta of Venus* by Anaïs Nin, the stories unfold with a deliberate pace that allows for the exploration of emotions and sensations, illustrating that even in erotica, the journey can be as important as the destination. Your stories can follow this model, balancing the urgency of desire with moments of introspection and connection.

In blending plot with erotic elements, your story needs to navigate the waters of narrative and arousal without sacrificing one for the other. Consider *Macho Sluts* by Pat Califia, a collection that weaves together compelling narratives with explicit scenes. Each story is a narrative, with the erotic elements enhancing rather than overshadowing the plot. This balance is crucial in crafting stories that remain engaging and stimulating throughout.

Creating compelling characters in erotica involves more than detailing their sexual preferences; it requires imbuing them with a sense of realism and complexity. *Crash* by J.G. Ballard is an example where characters are driven by their fetishistic desires. Yet, these desires are integral to their complex identities and the narrative's exploration of the intersection between technology, sex, and violence. Your characters should similarly be multifaceted, with their erotic desires intertwined with their personal growth and story arc.

Building sexual tension is not just about the physical inter-actions but the emotional and psychological dance leading up to them. In *Little Birds* by Anaïs Nin, the tension often lies in the unspoken, anticipation, and taboo, making the eventual consummation all the more intense. Your writing should layer these moments of anticipation, crafting scenes where desire builds in the space between words and actions.

The pacing of erotic scenes in your story can take its cues from *The Tropic of Cancer* by Henry Miller, where the narrative doesn't shy away from explicit content but inte-grates it seamlessly into the broader tapestry of the protago-nist's life and reflections. This approach shows that erotica can maintain a brisk pace without sacrificing depth, weaving erotic moments into a larger narrative that speaks to the human condition.

Your plot should serve as more than just a backdrop for erotic encounters; it should be a vessel for character devel-opment and thematic exploration. *Venus in Furs* by Leopold von Sacher-Masoch presents a narrative deeply intertwined with themes of power, submission, and desire, where the erotic elements serve to deepen the reader's understanding of the characters and their complex relationship. Aim to craft a plot that does more than connect erotic scenes—it should elevate them, adding layers of meaning and emotion.

In considering your audience, remember that the appetite for erotica varies widely. Books like *Fanny Hill* by John

Cleland have endured not just for their erotic content but for their historical and literary value, reminding us that readers seek a range of experiences in erotica. Some may crave the immediacy and intensity of sexual encounters, while others might appreciate the build-up and emotional layers leading to those moments.

When weaving erotic scenes into your narrative, look to *Peyton Place* by Grace Metalious, which, while not traditional erotica, integrates sexual themes and scenes into a broader narrative, challenging societal norms and expectations. This integration shows how erotic content can contribute to the story's thematic depth and character development, offering readers a more engaging experience.

Secondary characters and subplots can enrich your erotic narrative, offering new perspectives on desire and intimacy. In *The Story of the Eye* by Georges Bataille, the erotic escapades of the protagonists are mirrored and contrasted by the actions of secondary characters, adding depth and breadth to the exploration of sexuality. Use these elements to create a richer, more complex world within your stories.

The setting and atmosphere can amplify the erotic tension in your narrative. *Secretary* by Mary Gaitskill uses the mundane setting of an office to heighten the erotic charge between the characters, proving that the right atmosphere can turn even the most ordinary settings into a crucible for desire. Consider how your settings can add to the tension and mood of your scenes.

Dialogue in erotic scenes should do more than just convey desire; it should reveal character and build tension. *My Secret Life,* an anonymous Victorian memoir, showcases how dialogue can express the multifaceted nature of desire, from the tender to the taboo. Use dialogue to peel back layers of your characters, revealing their desires, fears, and personalities.

Themes of consent, power dynamics, and vulnerability are especially pertinent in erotica. *Exit to Eden* by Anne Rice explores these themes in depth, offering a narrative that is as much about the psychological aspects of BDSM as it is about the physical. Incorporate these themes thoughtfully into your stories to engage readers on a deeper level, encouraging them to reflect on the nature of desire and power.

Lastly, the revision process is crucial in erotica, as in any genre. Feedback from beta readers or editors who understand the finer points of erotica can help refine your narrative, ensuring that your erotic scenes are both arousing and integral to the story. Use this feedback to polish your scenes, ensuring they serve the narrative and character development, making your story hot and unforgettable.

Your journey as an erotic writer is about blending the visceral with the emotional, the physical with the psychological. Drawing inspiration from the works mentioned, you can craft stories that arouse and provoke thought and resonate with readers on a deeper level.

Chapter 7

Incorporating Tropes

Tropes serve as the foundation upon which many captivating narratives are built. Understanding how to implement these tropes effectively can elevate your writing, drawing readers into a world where desire and fantasy intertwine seamlessly. Here's a closer look at various tropes within erotica and strategies for their implementation:

The Forbidden Affair

Erotica thrives on the allure of the forbidden, such as affairs that defy social norms or personal commitments. To implement this trope, create a context that heightens the stakes—such as a relationship between a boss and their employee or step-siblings caught in a taboo romance. The key is to explore the emotional and psychological conflict that arises from the affair, making readers empathize with characters even as they transgress boundaries.

Dominance and Submission

This trope delves into power dynamics within sexual relationships, exploring themes of control, surrender, and consent. When writing D/S scenarios, establish clear boundaries and communication between characters to emphasize the consensual nature of their relationship. Incorporate scenes that explore both the physical aspects of dominance and submission and the emotional trust and connection that underpin them.

First Time Discoveries

The journey of sexual discovery is a potent narrative device. Characters may explore their sexuality for the first time, uncover hidden desires, or experiment with new partners or practices. To effectively use this trope, focus on the character's emotional growth, detailing their fears, curiosities, and eventual acceptance or joy in discovery, making their journey relatable and compelling.

Secret Desires Unleashed

Characters harboring secret sexual desires or fetishes find themselves in situations where they can finally explore these hidden aspects of their sexuality. Implement this trope by gradually building up the character's internal conflict and desire, leading to a pivotal moment of revelation or opportunity that allows for unleashing these desires in a safe and consensual context.

Power Plays

This trope involves characters engaging in psychological and sexual power games, often with stakes that extend beyond the bedroom. To write this, establish a context where power is a central theme—such as a competitive workplace or a historical setting with strict social hierarchies. Develop the push-and-pull dynamics between characters, showing how power shifts and evolves in their relationship.

Menage and Polyamory

Stories featuring multiple partners challenge conventional monogamous relationships, exploring the complexities and joys of love and sex with more than one person. When implementing this trope, focus on communication and consent among all parties. Highlight the emotional and logistical challenges they face and the unique bond and satisfaction that comes from their arrangement.

Transformation and Healing

Erotica often depicts characters undergoing transformation or healing through their sexual experiences. This trope can be implemented by pairing characters with contrasting experiences or backgrounds, allowing them to learn and grow from each other. Show how their sexual relationship contributes to their emotional healing or personal growth, making the transformation believable and satisfying.

Mystery and Suspense

Incorporating elements of mystery or suspense can add depth to erotic stories. Characters might explore their desires while entangled in a larger, dangerous plot. To use this trope effectively, weave the erotic elements seamlessly into the suspenseful narrative, ensuring that the sexual tension parallels the rising action of the plot.

Fantasy and Adventure

These stories are set in fantastical worlds or exotic locations and combine adventure with sensual exploration. Implementing this trope involves creating a rich, immersive world where sexual norms and practices differ from our own. Use the setting to challenge characters' preconceived notions of desire, allowing them to embark on a journey of erotic discovery alongside their adventure.

Role Reversal

Stories that play with the reversal of traditional sexual roles or dynamics offer fresh perspectives on desire and power. When writing such narratives, subvert expectations by placing characters in situations that force them to adopt unfamiliar roles. This trope can reveal new facets of characters' personalities and desires, deepening the reader's engagement with their journey.

The Seduction

Central to many erotica stories, the trope of seduction focuses on the art of enticing or being enticed. To craft compelling seduction scenes, build tension gradually through flirtation, innuendo, and the dance of mutual attraction. The seduction should feel like a natural culmination of the characters' interactions rather than a sudden event.

Age Gap

The dynamics of an age gap can introduce interesting power dynamics and emotional complexities. Focus on the mutual respect and attraction between the characters, addressing societal judgments they may face. Highlighting the personal growth that comes from their relationship can add depth to the trope, making it more than just about the age difference.

Rescue

Characters find themselves in difficult situations, only to be rescued by a partner, leading to an intense emotional and sexual connection. To implement this, ensure the rescue scenario feels integral to the plot and character development. The ensuing relationship should explore themes of vulnerability, gratitude, and the deep bond that forms through shared adversity.

Horror

Combines elements of fear and desire, exploring the darker sides of sexuality. When writing erotic horror, balance the arousal with genuine elements of suspense and fear, creating a tantalizing tension that plays on the primal instincts of the reader. The horror elements should enhance, not overshadow, the eroticism of the story.

The Affair

Often involves characters in committed relationships seeking fulfillment elsewhere. To effectively use this trope, delve into the emotional and ethical complexities of the affair. Focus on the reasons behind the characters' actions and the consequences they face, providing an exploration of infidelity and desire.

Forbidden Love

Explores relationships deemed unacceptable by society or circumstance, such as taboo liaisons or love between rivals. Emphasize the internal and external conflicts arising from the forbidden nature of the relationship, making readers root for the characters despite the odds.

Sexual Awakening

Follows a character's journey from sexual naivety to enlightenment. This trope is best implemented through a gradual exploration of sexuality, guided by a mixture of self-discovery and experiences with others. Show the transformative impact of this awakening on the character's life and relationships.

Captivity

Involves one character being held captive by another, leading to complex dynamics of power, consent, and eventual romance. Navigate this trope with care, focusing on the development of trust, consent, and mutual respect between the characters. The evolution from captivity to genuine emotional connection must be handled sensitively to avoid romanticizing non-consensual situations.

Comedy

Blends humor with eroticism, lightening the mood and providing a playful take on sexual encounters and relationships. Implement humor through witty dialogue, humorous situations, and characters' self-awareness. This trope can make erotica more accessible, breaking down barriers with laughter and allowing for a joyful exploration of sexuality.

Secret Societies

Erotica that revolves around exclusive clubs or societies, where members engage in secretive, often taboo sexual practices. These narratives can explore themes of power, secrecy, and the allure of the forbidden. Implementing this trope involves creating a compelling backdrop that entices readers with the promise of hidden desires and elite encounters, unveiling the mysteries and erotic adventures that lie within.

Bets and Games

Stories where characters engage in sexual acts as a result of bets, challenges, or games. This trope plays on the tension and excitement of risk-taking and the unexpected developments that can arise from such playful scenarios. Writers can use these situations to explore consent, boundaries, and the discovery of new desires, making the stakes more than just winning or losing.

Science Experiments

Narratives that involve characters participating in scientific studies related to sexuality, where experiments lead to unexpected arousal and connections. This setting allows for exploring themes like consent, the nature of attraction, and the boundaries between professional and personal. It's a unique way to delve into the psychology of desire under the guise of scientific inquiry.

Magic Spells and Potions

Utilizes elements of fantasy where characters use magical means to influence desire, attraction, or sexual performance. This trope opens avenues for stories about unintended consequences, the ethics of influence, and the true source of emotional connection. Writers can weave tales that question the power of magic versus the power of genuine human connection.

Dreams and Visions

Focuses on characters experiencing vivid erotic dreams or visions that influence their waking desires and actions. Such narratives allow for the exploration of subconscious desires, the blurring of reality and fantasy, and the impact of dreams on real-life relationships. Implementing this trope can add a layer of mystery and introspection to erotic stories.

Disguise and Masquerade

Involves characters attending masquerade balls or wearing disguises that free them to explore their sexuality anonymously. This setting offers a playground for exploring identity, the liberation from societal expectations, and the thrill of anonymous encounters. Writers can use disguises as a metaphor for the masks people wear and the desire to reveal one's true self.

Crossing the Line

Characters step out of their comfort zones or break their own rules for the sake of desire or love. This trope examines the growth and transformation that come from challenging personal boundaries, emphasizing the power of erotic encounters to change lives. It's a celebration of the bravery required to pursue true fulfillment.

Seducing the Enemy

Where characters initially at odds with each other find themselves drawn into an intense, erotic relationship. This trope delves into the complexities of attraction amid conflict, the fine line between love and hate, and the possibility of finding common ground in desire. The dynamic tension between the characters fuels the narrative's emotional and sexual charge.

Time Travel

Characters travel through time and engage in erotic encounters with people from different eras. This trope offers endless possibilities to explore historical sexual mores, the timeless nature of desire, and the impact of time on relationships. Writers can juxtapose the past and present to comment on the evolution of sexuality and romantic ideals.

Reluctant Partners

Involve characters who initially resist their attraction to each other due to external pressures, internal conflicts, or previous experiences. These stories often explore the tension between desire and resistance, eventually leading to a passionate resolution. This trope allows readers to experience the thrill of the chase and the satisfaction of eventual surrender.

Amnesia Lovers

Centers on a character who loses their memory, only to rediscover love and desire with a partner from their past or a new acquaintance. This setup explores themes of identity, the inherent nature of attraction, and the question of whether love can indeed be rekindled from scratch. It provides a fresh slate for characters to explore their desires without the baggage of their former selves.

Erotic Undercover Missions

Features characters who go undercover in sexually charged environments, such as sex clubs or erotic art scenes. The necessity to blend in leads to unexpected discoveries about their own desires and the complexities of the worlds they infiltrate. This trope allows for a deep dive into the exploration of sexual boundaries and the fluidity of identity.

Supernatural Bonds

Explores connections between characters that transcend the physical realm, such as soulmates marked by destiny or lovers bound by magical pacts. These stories delve into the power of connections that defy logical explanation, emphasizing the depth of emotional and physical ties that are predestined or supernaturally influenced.

Forced Proximity

Traps characters together in a confined space, compelling them to confront their desires and tensions head-on. Whether stranded in a snowstorm or locked in a safe house, the forced closeness ignites sparks that may have otherwise remained dormant. This trope plays on the intensity that arises from shared vulnerability and unexpected intimacy.

Revenge Seduction

Sees a character setting out to seduce another as revenge, only to find themselves genuinely falling for their target. This narrative explores the transformation from calculated desire to sincere emotional connection, challenging characters to reconcile their initial motives with their evolving feelings.

Pretend Relationships

Start as arrangements for mutual benefit, where characters fake a romantic or sexual relationship, but the act becomes reality as genuine feelings develop. This trope examines the line between performance and authenticity, revealing how pretend affections can lead to real passion and love.

Transformation Fantasies

Involve characters undergoing physical or magical transformations that lead to new explorations of their sexuality. Whether becoming a supernatural creature or experiencing a change in physical appearance, these transformations challenge characters to embrace their altered selves and the desires that come with them.

Virtual Desires

Navigates the realm of online relationships and virtual reality, where characters explore their sexuality through digital means. This modern trope reflects contemporary issues of identity, privacy, and the genuine connections that can form in the digital age, offering a space for fantasy that's both safe and boundless.

Age of Enlightenment

Features characters discovering or rekindling their sexual selves later in life, challenging the misconception that passion fades with age. These narratives celebrate the wisdom, confidence, and openness that come with experience, offering stories of sexual awakening that inspire readers to embrace their desires at any stage of life.

Chapter 8

Diversifying your Narratives

Diversifying your narratives in erotica involves more than just adding characters from various backgrounds; it requires a deep understanding and respectful representation of those backgrounds. When incorporating LGBTQ+ themes, for instance, it's crucial to go beyond the surface level of sexual orientation. This means crafting characters with complex identities and experiences that reflect the real challenges and joys of LGBTQ+ lives. Exploring the novelties of relationships, whether they're same-sex, bisexual, pansexual, or involve transgender characters, demands sensitivity to the community's diversified experiences. Books like *"Call Me by Your Name"* by André Aciman have paved the way, offering profound insights into the complexities of desire and identity. Authors should strive to create stories that resonate authentically with LGBTQ+ readers, offering narratives that celebrate love and desire in all its forms while acknowledging the unique struggles faced by these communities.

Urban erotica, with its gritty, raw settings, offers a canvas to explore sexuality within the vibrant, often chaotic energy of city life. This genre provides an opportunity to delve into stories that combine the fast-paced, diverse backdrop of urban environments with the intimate, personal experiences of characters navigating their desires. Urban settings allow for a rich exploration of socio-economic factors, cultural diversity, and the unique challenges and opportunities that come with city living. For authors, this means creating characters as multifaceted as the cities they inhabit, from the high-powered executive to the struggling artist, each with their journeys. *"Addicted"* by Zane is a prime example, blending steamy encounters with deeper issues of addiction, infidelity, and the quest for personal fulfillment against an urban backdrop.

Interracial erotica offers a powerful avenue to explore the dynamics of desire across racial and ethnic lines, challenging societal norms and taboos. Crafting stories in this genre requires a thoughtful approach to racial dynamics, ensuring that relationships are portrayed with depth, respect, and authenticity. It's about highlighting the beauty and complexity of interracial relationships, addressing cultural differences and societal pressures while focusing on the universal aspects of attraction and love. Authors can draw inspiration from real-life experiences and stories, bringing to light the richness of interracial connections. *"The Color of Love"* by Sandra Kitt explores the relationship between a black woman and a white man and navigates the challenges they face from society and their families, providing a heart-felt look at love and prejudice.

African American erotica celebrates the Black community's sensuality, culture, and experiences. Writing in this genre offers an opportunity to delve into stories rich with cultural specificity, exploring themes of love, desire, and eroticism through the lens of Black experiences. Authors should aim to create narratives that are not only sexually empowering but also culturally resonant, reflecting the diversity within African American communities. This involves developing characters whose identities and stories are deeply rooted in their cultural background, offering readers both escapism and a reflection of their lives. *"Gettin' Buck Wild: Sex Chronicles II"* by Zane showcases this beautifully, offering stories that are both erotically and culturally charged.

Exploring BDSM in erotica from a diverse perspective involves more than just the dynamics of dominance and submission; it's about understanding and respecting the practices and boundaries within BDSM communities. Authors venturing into this territory should research and portray BDSM relationships with accuracy and sensitivity, avoiding stereotypes and acknowledging the trust and consent that form the foundation of these dynamics. Including characters from various backgrounds in BDSM narratives not only enriches the story but also broadens the representation within this genre. Stories like *"Fifty Shades of Grey"* by E.L. James have popularized BDSM, but there's a rich world beyond that, full of diverse experiences and practices waiting to be explored in more depth.

Body positivity in erotica is another crucial aspect of diversifying narratives. Celebrating bodies of all shapes, sizes, and abilities is essential, creating characters who are confident in their sexuality regardless of societal beauty standards. This approach challenges the narrow definitions of desire and attractiveness and resonates with a broader audience, offering stories where everyone can see themselves as desirable and loved. Erotica, which champions body positivity, not only empowers readers but also promotes a healthier, more inclusive understanding of beauty and desire.

Incorporating non-binary and genderqueer characters into erotica enriches the genre by challenging traditional gender roles and exploring a spectrum of gender identities and expressions. These characters must be fully realized individuals whose gender identity is an integral but not sole aspect of their character. This requires authors to engage with the experiences of non-binary and genderqueer communities, understanding the fluidity of gender and how it influences their characters' desires and relationships. Stories like *"Gender Outlaws: The Next Generation,"* edited by Kate Bornstein and S. Bear Bergman, though not strictly erotica, provide insight and inspiration for incorporating diverse gender experiences into erotic narratives.

The inclusion of disability in erotica narratives is a powerful way to challenge stereotypes and celebrate sexuality in all its forms. Characters with disabilities should be portrayed as complex individuals with desires and erotic experiences that are fulfilling and consensual. This representation is crucial for challenging the often-desexualized perceptions of disabled individuals, showing that physical or mental differences do not diminish the capacity for love, pleasure, and intimate connection. *"Thank You for Holding"* by Julia Kent and Elisa Reed is an example of a romance that includes disability with sensitivity, humor, and heat, offering a model for erotic writers to follow.

Age diversity in erotica also offers a broader spectrum of desire, moving beyond the focus on young characters to explore the sexual lives of those in middle age or older. These stories can provide a rich exploration of experiences, reflecting the depth and intensity of desire that persists throughout life. Authors can explore themes of rediscovery, enduring passion, and the complexities of love and desire later in life by including older characters. *"Autumn Leaves: Love So Deep"* by Candice Poarch features mature protagonists, offering readers a refreshing perspective on romance and desire that defies ageist stereotypes.

Cultural diversity in erotica broadens the genre's appeal and allows for a more inclusive exploration of desire and identity. By weaving stories that draw from a rich tapestry of cultural backgrounds, authors can illuminate how culture influences sexuality, relationships, and erotic expression. This diversity enriches the genre, offering a wider array of narratives that reflect the world's plurality. *"The Sexy Part of the Bible"* by Kola Boof explores sexuality within a specific cultural context, providing a vivid example of how erotica can celebrate cultural identity.

Exploring eroticism through the lens of mental health can offer profound insights into the complexities of desire and the human psyche. Narratives that address mental health challenges with empathy and depth can shed light on how these experiences intersect with sexuality, offering a deeper look at intimacy in this regard. Such stories can both destigmatize mental health issues and affirm the sexual agency of individuals navigating these challenges. *"Tender Is the Flesh"* by Agustina Bazterrica, though not a traditional erotica, delves into dark themes with psychological depth, offering a model for how erotic fiction might explore the intersections of desire and mental health.

The integration of polyamory and non-monogamous relationships into erotica reflects the growing recognition of diverse relationship structures. *"Polysecure"* by Jessica Fern. However, non-fiction provides valuable insights that can inform the portrayal of polyamorous relationships in erotic narratives, emphasizing security and attachment in multiple partnerships.

Chapter 9

Language and Imagery

Creating vivid, sensual scenes requires a delicate balance of language and imagery, inviting the reader into a world of heightened senses and emotions. Start by focusing on the details: the skin of fingertips, the warmth of breath, and the sound of something falling. These details build a tangible world, making the scene come alive in the reader's mind. Use language that evokes the senses, words that paint a picture so vivid the reader can almost touch, taste, and smell the scene you're creating.

Imagery is your ally in crafting sensual scenes. Employ metaphors and similes that draw from the natural world or everyday objects to describe the indescribable. Compare the curve of a lover's spine to the gentle slope of a hill at sunrise or the taste of a kiss to the first drop of wine from a newly opened bottle. These comparisons enrich your narrative and anchor the sensuality in experiences the reader can understand and appreciate.

The pacing of your language plays a crucial role in building tension and desire. Slow down when you describe a touch, a look, a feeling, allowing the reader to savor each moment as if they were experiencing it themselves. Then, quicken the pace as the scene escalates, mirroring the characters' increasing heart rates and the urgency of their desires. This ebb and flow of pacing mimics the natural rhythm of an intimate encounter, drawing the reader deeper into the experience.

Don't shy away from the power of dialogue in sensual scenes. What characters say or don't say can add layers of tension and desire. Whispered confessions, breathy demands, or even a shared silence can be as charged with eroticism as the most explicit descriptions. Use dialogue to reveal character desires, to build anticipation, and to break or heighten the tension at just the right moment.

Engage all the senses when crafting a sensual scene. Too often, writers focus solely on touch or sight, neglecting the power of smell, taste, and sound to evoke emotion and memory. Describe the scent of a lover's skin in the rain, the taste of salt on their lips, the sound of a whispered name in the dark. Engaging all the senses makes the scene more immersive and the experience more holistic.

Consider the setting of your sensual scene as another character in the narrative. Whether it's a rain-soaked garden, a dimly lit bedroom, or a secluded beach at sunset, the setting can enhance the mood and tone of the encounter. Use descriptive language to bring the setting to life, allowing it to influence and improve the scene's sensuality.

Be mindful of the emotional landscape of your characters during a sensual scene. Physical desire often intertwines many emotions—longing, vulnerability, power, release. Use internal monologue to give readers insight into your characters' feelings, making the scene both physically and emotionally vivid.

The choice of verbs is essential in sensual scenes. Opt for verbs that convey action and emotion with precision and intensity. Words like "caress," "tantalize," "devour," and "surrender" carry an inherent sensuality that can elevate the scene, making the actions feel more immediate and impactful.

Balance explicitness with implication. Sometimes, what is left unsaid or merely hinted at can be more sensual than the most detailed description. Use implication to invite readers to fill in the blanks with their imagination, making the scene more personal and engaging.

Remember that sensuality can be found in the smallest moments—the catch of breath before a kiss, the fleeting touch of a hand on bare skin, the lingering gaze that promises more. Though seemingly insignificant, these moments can be charged with desire and anticipation, making them pivotal in building a sensual atmosphere.

Play with temperature and texture in your descriptions. The contrast of hot and cold, smooth and rough, can add a tactile dimension to your scenes, making them more vivid. Describe the heat of a touch against skin and the roughness of a beard against the softness of a cheek to make the scene more dynamic and immersive.

Don't underestimate the power of rhythm in your writing. Just as in music, the rhythm of your language can influence the mood and tone of a sensual scene. Use shorter, staccato sentences to build tension and longer, flowing sentences to create moments of tenderness and connection.

Finally, revision is key to crafting the perfect sensual scene. Step back and read your scene aloud, or better yet, have someone else read it to you. This can help you catch awkward phrasings or missed opportunities to deepen the sensuality. Remember, crafting a vivid, sensual scene is as much about what you leave out as what you put in, allowing the reader's imagination to work alongside your words.

By focusing on language and imagery, engaging the senses, and paying attention to your characters' emotional and physical landscapes, you can create sensual scenes that captivate the reader and leave a lasting impression, making your narrative unforgettable.

Chapter 10

Believability and Arousal

As an erotica writer, your primary job extends beyond mere arousal; it's about creating a believable and immersive world that captivates the reader's senses and emotions. The foundation of such a narrative is thorough research and attention to detail. When you write about specific lifestyles or practices, particularly those within the BDSM community, accuracy and authenticity are crucial. Delve into the specifics of bondage techniques, the psychology of power exchange, and the importance of aftercare, grounding your story in reality even as it ventures into the realms of fantasy.

Details matter when setting your scene in a specific location or culture. If your encounter is set in a city you're not familiar with or involves cultural practices different from your own, it's essential to research those elements thoroughly. The internet, travel guides, and firsthand accounts can provide insight into a place's sights, sounds, and flavors. For instance, if your story is set in Paris, knowing the layout of the city, the ambiance of its neighborhoods, and French attitudes toward sexuality can make your narrative more engaging and authentic. This level of detail not only enriches the reader's experience but also embeds your erotic scenes in a tangible world.

Language and terminology in erotica must be carefully chosen and researched, particularly when describing anatomy, sexual acts, or emotions. Misused or outdated terms can jolt the reader out of the narrative, breaking the spell of arousal. Familiarize yourself with the language preferred by the communities you're writing about, whether it's the LGBTQ+ community; people engaged in BDSM or others.

The emotional depth of your characters is another area where research and detail pay off. Understanding human psychology and the complexities of sexual and emotional relationships allows you to create characters that feel real and relatable. Whether you're exploring the dynamics of a new relationship, the healing power of sexual intimacy, or the challenges of navigating desire, grounding your characters' experiences in psychological reality adds depth and believability to your narrative.

Medical and anatomical accuracy in your erotic scenes is not only a matter of believability but also of responsibility.

Misrepresenting the physical realities of sex can perpetuate myths and misunderstandings.

Historical erotica requires meticulous research to capture the period accurately. If your narrative is set in a historical context, details about clothing, language, social norms, and sexual attitudes of the time are essential. This research prevents anachronisms and immerses the reader in the historical setting, making the erotic elements more believable.

When writing about specific sexual fetishes or fantasies, understanding the psychology behind them can enhance the believability of your scenes. Many fetishes have deep psychological roots, and portraying them with sensitivity and accuracy can make your narrative more engaging and respectful. This approach also opens avenues for exploring your characters' emotional and psychological growth through their sexual experiences.

Technology and the digital world have transformed the landscape of human sexuality, offering new platforms for exploration and connection. If your story involves cybersex, online dating, or other digital encounters, staying current with the latest platforms and how people use them for sexual expression is vital. This attention to detail makes your story relevant but also speaks to the experiences of a digitally connected audience.

Erotic romance, while focusing on developing romantic relationships alongside erotic encounters, requires a deep understanding of emotional arcs and character development. Researching the stages of relationships, from the initial spark of attraction to the deepening of emotional bonds, can help you craft a believable and satisfying romantic journey that complements the erotic elements of your story.

The legal and social frameworks surrounding sexuality in different cultures and societies can add a layer of complexity to your narrative. Researching these aspects allows you to navigate sensitive topics with awareness and respect, whether you're writing about LGBTQ+ relationships in a conservative society or exploring the legality of BDSM practices. This approach enhances believability and situates your narrative within a broader social context.

Sensory details are crucial to creating vivid, immersive erotic scenes. Paying attention to the way things feel, taste, smell, sound, and look can transform a straightforward sex scene into an erotic experience that engages all the reader's senses. Research into the sensory aspects of different sexual activities, environments, and interactions can elevate your writing from simply arousing to genuinely transporting.

Cultural sensitivity is crucial when your narrative includes characters or settings from different cultures. Understanding cultural attitudes toward sex, gender roles, and relationships is essential for creating a respectful and authentic narrative.

This may involve consulting cultural consultants or sensitivity readers to ensure your portrayal does not perpetuate stereotypes or misrepresentations.

Psychological realism in your characters' sexual and emotional responses adds depth to your erotica. Researching and understanding the psychological effects of arousal, orgasm, and intimacy can help you depict these experiences more accurately and compellingly. This attention to the psychological aspects of sex ensures that your characters' reactions and transformations are believable and relatable.

The believability of your story also depends on the internal consistency of the world you create. Even in fantasy or science fiction erotica, the rules of your world must be clear and adhered to throughout the story. Researching world-building techniques and ensuring that your narrative respects the internal logic of its setting can make even the most unbelievable erotic scenes feel real and possible within the context of your story.

Chapter 11

Avoiding Clichés and Common Pitfalls

Avoiding clichés and common pitfalls in erotic writing is crucial for creating fresh and engaging narratives. One common trope to steer clear of is the "inexperienced virgin" who is awakened to unimaginable pleasures by a more experienced partner. While this setup can be enticing, it's been overused to the point of becoming predictable. Instead, consider exploring characters with varied levels of experience, each bringing their own knowledge, desires, and insecurities to the encounter. This approach avoids cliché and allows for a more balanced exploration of sexuality.

Another pitfall is the over-reliance on physical descriptions at the expense of emotional depth. While detailed physicality is a key component of erotic writing, it shouldn't overshadow the emotional and psychological aspects of an encounter. Instead of focusing solely on the mechanics of sex, delve into the characters' internal experiences—their thoughts, feelings, and how the encounter changes them. This creates a more rounded and compelling narrative that resonates with readers on multiple levels.

The "millionaire dom" archetype, popularized by particular blockbuster series, has become a cliché that can limit the diversity of narratives in erotica. While wealth and power dynamics can be erotically charged, they're not the only frameworks for exploring dominance and submission. Consider settings or characters that break this mold, perhaps by exploring BDSM dynamics in everyday relationships or within communities rarely represented in mainstream erotica. This not only broadens the scope of your storytelling but also introduces readers to a broader range of erotic experiences.

Avoiding the trap of "love at first sight" as a precursor to erotic encounters can also enhance the believability and depth of your narratives. Instant attraction can be a powerful plot device, but genuine relationships—especially those involving significant emotional and sexual exploration—require development and conflict. Building tension through miscommunication, personal growth, or external obstacles can make the eventual consummation more satisfying for the reader.

Be wary of using sex as a cure-all for character development or plot resolution. While sexual encounters can be transformative, they shouldn't be presented as the sole solution to personal or relational issues. Characters should grow and evolve through a variety of experiences, with sex being one aspect of their journey. This avoids the pitfall of reducing erotica to a series of sexual panaceas and instead offers a more realistic portrayal of human relationships.

Incorporating diversity in your narratives goes beyond simply avoiding clichés; it's about challenging stereotypes and presenting a wide range of identities and experiences. Avoid reducing characters to their sexualities, ethnic backgrounds, or body types. Instead, present fully realized individuals whose erotic experiences are part of larger, multifaceted lives. This approach enriches your narrative and respects the diversity of your readership.

Dialogue in erotic scenes can often fall into the trap of being either too mechanical or unrealistically eloquent. Strive for a balance that reflects genuine communication between partners, including the awkward, uncertain, and playful moments. Authentic dialogue enhances the realism of a scene and can deepen the connection between characters—and between your story and its readers.

Another common pitfall is ignoring consent or blurring its lines for drama or tension. In contemporary erotica, it's essential to portray consent clearly and enthusiastically. This doesn't have to dampen the erotic charge of your scenes; instead, it can heighten the intimacy and trust between characters, making their encounters more charged and meaningful.

Finally, avoid the cliché of perfect, flawless characters engaging in flawless sex. Realism in erotic writing can be deeply arousing; showing characters navigating the messy, awkward aspects of sex—alongside its bliss—can enhance the eroticism of a scene. Incorporating moments of laughter, mishaps, or even disappointment can make your characters more relatable and their experiences more engaging.

By sidestepping these clichés and pitfalls, you elevate your erotic writing from the realm of the predictable to the compelling, offering narratives that captivate the imagination and resonate with the rich, complex reality of human sexuality.

Chapter 12

Are you part of the story?

The role of personal experiences and fantasies in crafting erotica is a delicate balancing act, one that requires the writer to navigate the fine line between authenticity and overindulgence. Individual experiences can serve as a rich wellspring of inspiration, lending a sense of realism and depth to erotic narratives. They allow writers to draw on genuine emotions, sensations, and dynamics, infusing their stories with the kind of detail and authenticity that resonates with readers. Yet, the challenge lies in transforming these personal experiences into narratives that engage a broader audience, ensuring the story transcends the purely personal to become universally compelling.

Incorporating personal fantasies into erotica offers a window into the writer's own desires, providing a unique and intimate perspective that can set a story apart. Fantasies can push the boundaries of conventional erotica, exploring uncharted territories of lust and pleasure. However, the artistry lies in weaving these fantasies into narratives inviting readers rather than alienating them with scenarios that feel too idiosyncratic or disconnected from their own experiences. The key is to find the universal appeal within the fantasy, making it as tantalizing to the reader as it is to the writer.

The question of whether the writer is part of the story or merely its creator is a nuanced one. On the one hand, injecting personal experiences and fantasies into the work can blur the lines between creator and creation, making the story a deeply personal expression of the writer's erotic landscape. On the other hand, the writer must also assume the role of a craftsman, shaping these raw materials into a story that stands on its own, independent of the writer's narrative. This requires detachment and objectivity, ensuring that the story serves the interests of the narrative and its characters rather than simply acting as a vehicle for the writer's exploration.

Knowing how to fantasize without overdoing it is a skill that erotic writers must hone. While erotica inherently invites readers into the realm of fantasy, there is a risk of crossing into the realm of the implausible or the excessively indulgent. To mitigate this, writers should ground their fantasies in emotional truth, creating scenarios that, perhaps adventurous or unconventional, resonate with genuine desires and fears. This connection to emotional reality helps keep the fantasy relatable, anchoring the narrative in the complexities of human desire.

Balancing the explicit with the implied is another strategy for managing the intensity of fantasy in erotica. Not every detail of a fantasy needs to be spelled out; sometimes, what is left to the imagination can be even more arousing. This approach allows readers to fill in the blanks with their own desires, making the story more interactive and personalized. It also prevents the narrative from becoming overwhelmed by the writer's specific vision, maintaining a space for the reader's fantasy life to engage with the story.

The diversity of personal experiences and fantasies in erotica is what makes the genre so rich and varied. Writers should not shy away from exploring a wide range of desires and scenarios, even those deviating from personal experiences. Research, empathy, and imagination can help writers authentically portray experiences outside their own, broadening the scope of their narratives and inviting a broader audience to find resonance within their stories.

The ethical considerations of drawing from personal experiences and fantasies in erotica cannot be overlooked. Writers must navigate privacy, consent, and respect issues, particularly when incorporating elements from real-life encounters or relationships. This may involve altering details to protect identities or seeking permission from individuals who may recognize themselves in the narrative. Ethical writing practices ensure that personal inspirations enrich the story without compromising the dignity or privacy of those involved.

The interplay between fantasy and reality in erotica allows writers to explore deeper themes and messages. Beyond arousal, erotica can probe questions of identity, power, intimacy, and liberation. Personal experiences and fantasies, when thoughtfully integrated, can elevate the narrative from mere titillation to a meaningful exploration of what it means to desire and be desired.

For writers, integrating personal experiences and fantasies into their work requires courage and vulnerability. Sharing one's erotic imagination with the world can be a daunting prospect. Still, it is also an act of artistic expression that can connect with readers in profound and unexpected ways. This emotional risk-taking is part of what makes erotica a unique and powerful genre.

Feedback from readers can be invaluable in understanding how personal fantasies translate in a broader context. Whether through reviews, social media, or direct communication, engaging with reader responses can offer insights into what resonates, provokes, and falls flat. This feedback loop can inform future writing, helping writers fine-tune their balance of personal experience and universal appeal.

Ultimately, the role of personal experiences and fantasies in erotica is not a binary choice between being part of the story or merely writing it. It's about weaving elements of the self into the fabric of the narrative in ways that enrich and deepen the reader's experience. The writer's challenge is to remain deeply connected to the material and sufficiently detached to serve the story's needs, ensuring that the personal is always in service of the greater narrative.

In conclusion, navigating the use of personal experiences and fantasies in erotica is a complex, nuanced process that requires sensitivity, creativity, and a keen awareness of the reader's experience. By striking the right balance, writers can craft stories that are arousing and meaningful, offering readers a window into the vast landscape of human desire.

Chapter 13

Finding your Voice

Finding one's voice is a journey that many successful authors have navigated, each with their own experiences and insights.

Anne Rice, under the pseudonym A.N. Roquelaure, for instance, ventured into erotic literature with her *"Sleeping Beauty"* series. Rice has shared in interviews how embracing her sexual explorations on page allowed her to discover a voice that was both daring and unapologetically sensual. Her advice to new authors often emphasizes the importance of honesty in writing, suggesting that the most authentic voice emerges when writers are true to their passions and fears.

Zane, the pseudonym of Kristina Laferne Roberts, who revolutionized African American erotica, has spoken about the liberating experience of self-publishing her work. She found her voice by writing stories that she felt were missing in the literary world—stories that combined steamy scenes with deeper narratives of personal growth and empowerment. Zane's journey underscores the significance of writing what you are passionate about, even if it means creating your path in the industry. Her success is a testament to staying true to one's vision and voice, regardless of mainstream notoriety.

E.L. James, author of the *"Fifty Shades of Grey"* series, often discusses how her writing began as a personal project, a way to explore her own sexual fantasies. James' transition from fan fiction writer to best-selling author is a powerful reminder that finding one's voice can sometimes mean embracing and transforming one's indulgences into compelling narratives for a wider audience. Her experience highlights the value of writing for oneself first, an approach that can lead to unexpected and profound connections with readers worldwide.

Chuck Tingle, a unique voice in erotic literature known for his humorous and often surreal take on the genre, has built a successful career by embracing the absurd and the profound. Tingle's approach to erotica, including titles featuring dinosaur billionaires and sentient objects, demonstrates the vast possibilities for authors to let their imaginations and idiosyncrasies guide their writing. His advice often includes encouraging writers to find what makes them different and lean into it, showcasing that a distinctive voice can emerge from the most unexpected places.

Sylvia Day, the author behind the *"Crossfire"* series, often speaks about the evolution of her writing voice over time. Day's journey from writing historical and paranormal romances to becoming a leading name in contemporary erotic romance illustrates how finding one's voice can be an ongoing process of exploration and refinement. She emphasizes the importance of reading widely and writing consistently, suggesting that exposure to different styles and the discipline of daily writing can help hone a unique voice.

Tiffany Reisz, known for her *"Original Sinners"* series, credits her distinctive voice to her willingness to tackle themes and subjects others might shy away from. Reisz often discusses how her background in theology and her interest in the complexities of human desire has shaped her approach to erotica. Her work blends deep emotional narratives with eroticism and showcases how an author's unique interests and knowledge can inform and enrich their voice.

Bella Andre, a successful self-published erotic romance author, often shares how her experience in the music industry influenced her writing voice. Andre's stories, known for their emotional depth and sensual scenes, reflect her belief in the power of rhythm and mood in storytelling. Her transition from songwriting to novel writing underscores the idea that finding one's voice can involve drawing on one's experiences and passions outside the literary world.

Madeline Miller, though not primarily an erotica author, has been celebrated for the sensual and emotional depth in her retellings of classical myths, such as *"The Song of Achilles."* Miller has spoken about the importance of empathy in her writing process, suggesting that deeply understanding her characters' desires and motivations has helped her find her voice. Focusing on the emotional truth of her characters' experiences, this approach offers valuable insight into how empathy and connection can shape an author's narrative voice.

Radclyffe, a prolific writer of lesbian erotica and romance, has often discussed the significance of writing stories that reflect her own experiences and the realities of the LGBTQ+ community. She emphasizes the importance of authenticity in creating a voice that resonates with readers, suggesting that accurate representation involves both the joys and challenges of queer lives. Radclyffe's success highlights how a voice grounded in personal and community truths can create powerful, relatable narratives.

Neil Gaiman, although not an erotica author, offers advice pertinent to writers across genres: *"Start telling the stories that only you can tell."* Gaiman's encouragement to embrace one's unique experiences, interests, and imagination in storytelling is a universal call to writers seeking their voice.

His reminder that authenticity and originality are key to captivating narratives is a guiding principle for erotica authors navigating the intimate and diverse landscapes of human desire.

These anecdotes from successful erotica and romance authors illuminate the varied paths to finding one's voice in erotica. Whether through embracing personal fantasies, drawing on unique experiences, or steadfastly writing one's truth, the journey to discovering and refining one's narrative voice is deeply personal and endlessly rewarding.

Chapter 14

Balancing Explicit Content with Tasteful Narrative

Balancing explicit content with tasteful narrative is an art form that requires sensitivity, hinting, and a deep understanding of the genre's dual aim: to arouse and to tell a compelling story. Successful writers navigate this balance by understanding that the explicitness serves the narrative, enhancing the emotional and psychological development of the characters. It's about using explicit scenes to deepen the reader's understanding of the characters, their desires, and their relationships rather than including such content for its own sake.

A key strategy in achieving this balance is the judicious use of language. Writers can choose words that evoke sensuality and desire without resorting to vulgarity unless it serves a specific purpose in character development or plot. The elegance of language in both erotica and erotic romance lies in its ability to paint vivid pictures in the reader's mind, using metaphor and simile to describe intimate acts in a fresh and evocative way. This approach maintains the tastefulness of the narrative and enriches the reader's experience by engaging their imagination and tantalizing their insides.

The pacing of the narrative plays a crucial role in balancing explicit content. By building tension slowly, weaving in moments of anticipation and longing, writers can create a tasteful narrative filled with arousal. This slow-burn approach makes the explicit scenes feel earned, a natural culmination of the characters' emotional journey rather than gratuitous additions to the plot. It's the narrative equivalent of foreplay, setting the stage for a more impactful and meaningful exploration of sexuality.

Character development is another vital aspect of balancing explicitness with tastefulness. Characters in erotic romance should be fully realized individuals with passions, fears, and motives beyond the bedroom. When explicit scenes are grounded in the characters' emotional landscapes, they become a powerful tool for exploring vulnerability, intimacy, and transformation. This depth of character ensures that the erotic content feels integral to the story rather than excessive or exploitative.

Contextualizing the explicit scenes within a broader narrative arc is essential for maintaining tastefulness. Erotic Romance, which explores themes of love, power, identity, or healing, can provide a rich framework within which the sexual content serves a larger purpose. When explicit scenes are woven into a narrative that deals with complex human experiences, they gain emotional and thematic weight, elevating the story from mere titillation to a hinted exploration of the human condition.

Incorporating diversity in perspectives and experiences can also help balance explicit content with a tasteful narrative. Erotica & Erotic Romance, which embraces a wide range of sexualities, body types, and relationship dynamics, reflects the complexity and richness of human desire. By challenging stereotypes and presenting a broad spectrum of erotic experiences, writers can create stories that feel inclusive, respectful, and genuinely erotic.

The emotional aftermath of explicit scenes is a crucial component of a balanced narrative. Addressing the consequences, revelations, and transformations that follow intimate encounters adds depth to the story, ensuring that the content is momentary and has lasting implications for the characters and the plot. This attention to the aftermath lends credibility to the narrative and invites readers to resonate with the story more deeply.

Feedback from readers and sensitivity readers can be invaluable in striking the right balance between explicitness and tastefulness. By listening to diverse perspectives on how the content is perceived, writers can fine-tune their narratives to ensure they resonate with readers as intended. This open dialogue with the audience highlights the collaborative nature of storytelling, where the writer's vision meets the reader's imagination.

The key to balancing explicit content with tasteful narrative lies in the writer's intention. When explicit scenes are crafted with care to illuminate, challenge, or celebrate aspects of the human experience, they transcend mere arousal to become art. Erotica, at its best, is a celebration of human connection, vulnerability, and the infinite variations of desire. Writers can create arousing and passionate narratives by approaching explicit content with creativity and a deep commitment to storytelling.

Chapter 15

Where to Market your Book

Navigating the intricate landscape of marketing erotica necessitates a strategic blend of direct engagement and savvy promotion, especially given the genre's unique challenges. A particularly effective avenue is leveraging specialized erotica newsletters like "Shameless Book Deals," which cater directly to an audience craving steamy reads. This targeted approach ensures your book lands in the inboxes of readers who prefer erotica, significantly increasing the likelihood of engagement. The direct nature of email marketing allows for personalized recommendations, making it a potent tool in the erotica author's arsenal. Such platforms offer a direct line to an interested audience and allow authors to highlight their work amidst a curated selection of erotica, enhancing visibility and appeal.

Smashwords emerges as a leading digital publishing marketplace for erotica authors, thanks to its inclusive policy towards adult content and its distribution network across multiple ebook retailers. This platform stands out for its author-friendly tools and features, such as detailed analytics and marketing options, which empower writers to reach a wider audience. For erotica authors, Smashwords is invaluable, offering a space where their work can be freely published and promoted without the stringent content restrictions found on other platforms. Additionally, the platform's promotional tools, like coupons and author interviews, offer unique ways to engage with readers and drive sales. By leveraging Smashwords, authors can ensure their erotica reaches readers across many digital bookstores, broadening their exposure. **(As of date, Draft2Digital is now the owner of Smashwords.)**

Amazon's KDP Kindle Countdown Deals present a lucrative opportunity for erotica authors to entice readers with time-limited discounts. This marketing strategy boosts the book's visibility within the crowded Kindle marketplace and creates a sense of urgency among potential readers, encouraging quicker purchasing decisions. The temporal nature of these deals, highlighted on the book's Amazon page, attracts price-conscious readers looking for quality erotica at a discount. Moreover, authors can amplify their promotion through social media and newsletters, maximizing the reach and impact of the countdown deal. Utilizing Kindle Countdown Deals effectively can increase sales and rankings, providing a significant visibility boost on one of the world's largest book-selling platforms.

Specialized erotica newsletter promo companies like Excite Spice offer tailored marketing services directly targeting erotica enthusiasts. These companies understand the nuances of promoting adult content and can navigate the challenges of reaching readers in a genre often subject to advertising restrictions. By featuring your book in a themed newsletter, your work is presented to readers actively seeking new erotica, ensuring a higher engagement rate. This targeted approach is invaluable for authors looking to connect with a dedicated and engaged audience, making these promo companies an essential tool in the erotica author's marketing toolkit. Collaborating with such services streamlines the promotional process, allowing authors to focus on writing while still reaching a wide audience.

While social media platforms often impose restrictions on adult content, Twitter and Reddit provide more lenient spaces for erotica authors to engage with their community. These platforms host vibrant discussions and fan communities dedicated to erotica and romance genres, allowing authors to share their work, participate in discussions, and connect with potential readers. By engaging authentically with these communities, authors can build a loyal following and drive interest in their books. Sharing teasers, excerpts, or behind-the-scenes content can entice readers, creating anticipation for upcoming releases. Navigating these platforms with tact and engaging content can turn them into valuable tools for building visibility and establishing a direct line to readers.

An author's website or blog dedicated to erotica serves as the cornerstone of an effective marketing strategy. This digital hub allows authors to showcase their catalog, share exclusive content, and interact with readers through comments and newsletters. A well-maintained site can attract new readers through search engines and retain existing fans by informing them about new releases and author news. Additionally, integrating an email sign-up form on the website enables authors to grow their mailing list, a crucial asset for direct marketing efforts. By providing a mix of engaging content, from short stories to insights into the writing process, authors can create a loyal community around their work.

Email marketing remains one of the most direct and effective ways to reach erotica readers. Building an email list allows authors to send updates, promotions, and exclusive content directly to their audience's inboxes. This method fosters a personal connection with readers, encouraging loyalty and repeat readership. By segmenting their list based on reader preferences or past purchases, authors can tailor their messages to specific audience subsets, increasing relevance and engagement. Effective email marketing campaigns can significantly boost visibility for new releases and backlist titles alike.

Online forums and discussion groups offer a fertile ground for authors to sow interest in their erotica. Platforms like Goodreads host myriad groups where fans of erotica gather to share recommendations and discuss their favorite reads. Participating in these groups allows authors to understand current trends and reader preferences and provides an opportunity to promote their work subtly. Engaging in discussions, providing book recommendations, and becoming an active community member can elevate an author's profile and attract readers to their work. This grassroots approach to marketing fosters organic growth and builds a dedicated reader base over time.

Paid advertising, though challenging due to content restrictions, remains a viable option for reaching erotica readers. Specific ad networks and websites cater to adult content, offering targeted advertising opportunities. These platforms allow authors to reach readers specifically interested in erotica, making for highly effective campaigns. Making compelling ads that comply with platform guidelines while enticing readers is key to success. When done wisely, Investing in paid advertising can yield a significant return in book sales and new reader acquisition. **(This is nearly impossible on Amazon. Sometimes, you can squeak an erotic book in if you do some things like changing the title, cover, & blurb. I've done it with Amazon and have**

two Erotica books currently running. It's definitely on a case-by-case basis. Bookbub does allow ads on its platform. Facebook and TikTok are big nopes!)

Collaborations with other erotica authors can amplify marketing efforts exponentially. Joining forces for anthology projects (boxsets), bundle deals, or cross-promotions can introduce your work to the audiences of your collaborators, expanding your reach. These partnerships provide exposure and foster a sense of community among authors and readers alike. Sharing promotional responsibilities and leveraging each author's platform and audience can increase visibility and sales. This strategy underscores the power of community in the erotica genre, where authors can support and uplift one another.

Offering free content, such as short stories or sample chapters, can be a powerful incentive for new readers. This "try before you buy" approach allows readers to understand an author's style and storytelling before committing to a purchase. Free content can be particularly effective when introducing a series, enticing readers to purchase subsequent books to continue the story. Hosting free content on your website or platforms like Medium and Literotica can increase your visibility and attract a following. This strategy leverages the allure of freebies to build an audience and drive interest in paid titles. **(Be careful. You have individuals who scrape the net and republish these stories on other platforms.)**

Utilizing book promotion sites and services that cater to the erotica genre can significantly boost a book's visibility. Platforms like BookBub, which offers a dedicated Erotic Romance category, reach millions of readers actively seeking new books. Being featured on such a platform can lead to a surge in sales and new fans. While getting selected for a feature can be competitive, the potential exposure makes it a worthwhile goal for erotica authors. Often amplified by the platform's extensive reach, these promotions can be a game-changer in an author's promotional strategy.

Engaging with readers through live readings, virtual book clubs, or writing workshops can create a personal connection beyond the page. These interactions offer readers a glimpse into the author's world, making the stories and characters even more compelling. Whether in person or virtually, talking about your work live allows authors to showcase their work, answer questions, and build a rapport with their audience. This level of engagement can turn casual readers into loyal fans, creating a community around the author's work.

Understanding and capitalizing on trends within the erotica genre can inform and enhance marketing strategies. Keeping abreast of what readers enjoy, from thematic trends to popular tropes, can help authors tailor their promotional messages and target their advertising more effectively. This might involve aligning book covers, descriptions, or marketing campaigns with current trends to appeal to reader interests. By staying in tune with the erotica market, authors can position their books to meet reader demand, increasing the likelihood of success.

Marketing an erotica book requires a multifaceted approach that respects the genre's unique challenges and opportunities. Authors can effectively reach and expand their audience by employing a mix of direct marketing, community engagement, strategic promotions, and trend analysis. Whether through newsletter promotions, strategic use of platforms like Smashwords and KDP, or engaging directly with readers, the goal remains to connect with readers meaningfully, fostering a community of fans eager for your next release.

Chapter 16

Resources for Erotica Authors

For erotica writers navigating the complexities of crafting and marketing their work, a wealth of resources is available to support their journey. From online communities to writing guides, these tools can offer invaluable insights, networking opportunities, and exposure.

One essential resource is the Erotica Readers & Writers Association (ERWA). Offering a comprehensive suite of resources, ERWA provides everything from writing advice and market listings to forums where writers can connect with peers. Its commitment to supporting erotica writers of all levels makes it a cornerstone of the community. The association's website hosts articles on craft, genre-specific writing challenges, and updates on publishing opportunities, making it a one-stop shop for both novice and experienced authors.

Writing workshops and courses tailored explicitly for erotica can be instrumental in honing one's craft. Websites like LitReactor and Coursera offer classes taught by seasoned authors, covering topics from character development to building tension. These courses provide practical writing tips and foster a community of writers who can offer feedback and support. These educational opportunities can elevate an author's writing, ensuring their work resonates with audiences.

Networking opportunities at writers' conferences and erotica-specific events can be invaluable. Conferences like the Romance Writers of America annual convention often host workshops and panels dedicated to erotica, providing a platform for learning and networking. Attending such events can connect writers with publishers, agents, and other authors, opening doors to collaborations and publishing opportunities. The face-to-face interactions at these gatherings can foster lasting professional relationships and offer insights that are difficult to gain through online research alone.

Online forums such as Reddit's r/Erotica and r/Eroticauthors subreddits offer a space for writers to share experiences, seek advice, and discuss industry trends. These platforms allow for real-time interaction with a global community of erotica writers, offering diverse perspectives and solutions to common challenges. Participating in these forums can provide support, inspiration, and a sense of belonging to a broader writing community.

Erotica writing guides, such as "How to Write Hot Sex: Tips from Multi-Published Erotic Romance Authors" by Shoshanna Evers, offer genre-specific insights and tips. These guides can help writers navigate the nitty-gritty of crafting compelling, sensual scenes and developing engaging storylines. By learning from successful authors, writers can avoid common pitfalls and refine their approach.

Submission trackers like Duotrope and The (Submission) Grinder are invaluable for writers seeking publication. These tools offer detailed information on publishers and literary magazines, including response times and acceptance rates. For erotica authors looking to submit their work, these trackers can streamline the process, helping to identify the best fit for their stories.

While sometimes challenging due to content restrictions, social media platforms can still be powerful tools for erotica writers. Twitter, in particular, has a vibrant community of erotica authors and readers. Using hashtags like #erotica and #eroticawriters can help authors connect with their audience, share their work, and stay informed about industry news.

Erotica-specific publishers, such as Ellora's Cave and Cleis Press, offer submission opportunities tailored to erotica writers.

Researching and targeting publishers that specialize in erotica can increase the chances of acceptance and ensure that the work reaches an interested audience. Websites of these publishers often provide submission guidelines and tips for authors, making them a crucial resource for those looking to publish.

Book promotion sites like The Fussy Librarian and BookBub offer categories for erotica, allowing authors to reach readers specifically interested in the genre. These platforms can significantly boost a book's visibility, driving sales and attracting new readers. Utilizing these promotional opportunities can be a game-changer for authors looking to market their erotica effectively.

Writer's market guides, although more general, can still offer valuable information on publishers, agents, and magazines that accept erotica submissions. Publications like "Writer's Market" include detailed listings and advice on crafting query letters and proposals, making them useful for authors navigating the submission process.

Author websites and blogs are both a promotional tool and a platform for sharing insights about writing erotica. Successful erotica authors often blog about their writing process, industry news, and tips for aspiring writers. These personal websites can also host mailing lists, further engaging readers and building a dedicated fanbase.

Erotica writing contests can provide exposure and credibility for authors. Competitions like the annual Smut

Marathon challenge writers to create compelling erotica under specific constraints, offering a platform for showcasing talent and gaining recognition.

Peer critique groups, available through platforms like Scribophile and Critique Circle, offer a space for receiving constructive feedback on erotica manuscripts. Engaging with fellow writers in a supportive environment can improve the quality of the work and provide new insights into the craft of writing erotica.

Finally, online courses on digital marketing and self-publishing can be invaluable for erotica authors looking to navigate the business side of writing. Platforms like Udemy and Skillshare offer courses tailored to authors **(in general)**, covering topics from social media marketing to self-publishing on platforms like Amazon KDP. **(Don't get suckered into the gurus' of self-publishing. Find out who is really doing the work. Do your diligence before hiring anyone. Not every marketer is a bestselling author, and the opposite.)**

By leveraging these resources, erotica writers can improve their craft, find workarounds in the complexities of the publishing industry, and connect with a community of like-minded authors and publishers. The journey of writing erotica is unique and filled with creative and professional challenges, but with the right tools and support, you can find success.

Chapter 17

Glossary

BDSM: This encompasses practices involving bondage and discipline, dominance and submission, and sadism and masochism. In erotica, BDSM explores the power dynamics and trust between partners, often highlighting the deep emotional connections that can form from these interactions.

Consent: A fundamental aspect of erotica, consent refers to the explicit agreement between participants to engage in the sexual acts described. It underscores the importance of safety, respect, and mutual desire in all erotic encounters, serving as a cornerstone for ethical depictions of sexuality.

Submissive: Characters who willingly give up control to a dominant partner in a sexual or romantic context. This role is defined by a range of behaviors from following commands to engaging in complex power exchanges, highlighting the desire for emotional release, pleasure, or intimacy through submission.

Kink: Refers to sexual practices or desires that deviate from conventional norms, encompassing activities like bondage, discipline, fetishes, and role-playing. Erotica often delves into various kinks to explore the intricacies of desire and pleasure beyond traditional sexual expressions.

Taboo: Themes or scenarios considered socially unacceptable or forbidden, such as incest fantasies or extreme age play. Erotica that explores taboo topics pushes the boundaries of conventional desire, often provoking a heightened state of arousal due to the prohibitive nature of the content.

Master/Slave: A dynamic within BDSM characterized by a total power exchange, with one person (the Master) taking complete control and the other (the Slave) yielding all power. These relationships are built on consensual agreements and explore the depth of dominance and submission through strict roles and protocols.

Virgin: Narratives centered around characters who have not experienced sexual intercourse, focusing on their first sexual encounters. These stories explore awakening, discovery, and the emotional journey toward sexual initiation, often framed within a context of learning or exploration.

Exhibitionism: Involves characters who derive pleasure and arousal from being watched by others during sexual acts. This kink explores the thrill of exposure and being seen, often challenging notions of privacy and societal norms regarding sexuality.

Voyeurism: The counterpart to exhibitionism, voyeurism describes characters who find sexual satisfaction in watching others engage in sexual acts. This dynamic plays on the tension between the desire to observe and the taboo nature of watching, offering a voyeuristic pleasure to the reader as well.

Fetish: Refers to a sexual fixation on a non-genital body part, object, or specific situation that becomes necessary for sexual satisfaction. Erotica often explores a range of fetishes, delving into the psychological and emotional aspects that make these fixations erotically charged for the characters.

Power Exchange: A BDSM term that describes the dynamic in which one partner willingly gives up control to another, establishing a dominant/submissive relationship. This exchange is central to many erotic narratives, exploring the trust, communication, and emotional depth required to navigate these relationships.

Role-Playing: Involves characters adopting specific roles or personas during sexual encounters, often as a form of escapism or to fulfill fantasies. This practice can range from simple scenarios to complex setups, allowing characters to explore different aspects of their sexuality in a controlled environment.

Sensory Deprivation: A practice within BDSM where one partner's senses are deliberately restricted to heighten other sensations. Common methods include blindfolding or using headphones to block sound, intensifying the experience of touch, and other remaining senses during sexual play.

Sadism and Masochism: Sadism refers to deriving pleasure from inflicting pain or humiliation, while masochism involves finding pleasure in receiving pain or humiliation. These dynamics, integral to the BDSM community, explore the complex interplay between pain and pleasure.

Asphyxiation: A highly risky and controversial practice that involves restricting a partner's breathing for the purposes of sexual arousal. While it appears in erotica, it's often accompanied by warnings about its dangers, highlighting the importance of consent, safety, and informed practice.

Aftercare: The practice of providing physical and emotional care and support after a BDSM scene. Aftercare is essential for re-establishing trust and ensuring the well-being of all participants, emphasizing the depth of care and responsibility inherent in BDSM relationships.

Non-Con/Dub-Con: Short for non-consent and dubious consent, these terms describe scenarios where consent is either not given or is ambiguous. While these themes can be explored in erotica, they are approached with sensitivity and often include discussions about fantasy versus reality, highlighting the importance of informed consent in real-life sexual encounters.

Swinging: Refers to a lifestyle in which individuals or couples consensually engage in sexual activities with others outside their primary relationship. Erotica exploring this theme delves into the dynamics of jealousy, trust, and sexual exploration within the context of swinging.

Orgasm Denial: A practice often found in BDSM contexts where a person is brought to the brink of orgasm but is intentionally prevented from reaching climax. This technique emphasizes control and heightens sexual tension, often leading to more intense experiences when release is finally granted.

Cuckolding: A scenario involving a person, typically a man, who derives pleasure from watching their partner engage in sexual activity with someone else. This kink explores themes of humiliation, dominance, and voyeurism, challenging traditional notions of monogamy and possessiveness.

Edging: The practice of approaching the edge of sexual climax but stopping short to prolong sexual activity. Edging can intensify eventual orgasms and is often used in erotica to build narrative tension and enhance the eroticism of a scene.

Polyamory: The practice of engaging in multiple romantic or sexual relationships with the consent of all parties involved. Erotica that explores polyamory delves into the complexities of love, jealousy, and communication in non-monogamous relationships, offering a look at alternative relationship structures.

Impact Play: A form of BDSM that involves striking the body for sexual gratification. Common tools include hands, paddles, whips, or canes. Impact play scenes in erotica explore the balance between pain and pleasure, trust, and the physical sensations that contribute to arousal.

Pegging: A sexual practice where a person, typically a woman, penetrates a male partner's anus with a strap-on dildo. In erotica, pegging challenges traditional gender roles and explores themes of role reversal, power dynamics, and anal pleasure.

Hypnosis: The use of hypnosis techniques to induce arousal or enhance sexual experiences. This practice can involve suggestions of relaxation, heightened sensitivity, or fantasy scenarios, offering a unique avenue for exploring control and desire in erotic fiction.

Tease and Denial: Similar to orgasm denial, this practice involves teasing a partner to the brink of sexual climax but repeatedly preventing release. It heightens anticipation and desire, creating a dynamic of control and submission that can be deeply erotic.

Public Play: Engaging in sexual acts in semi-public or public spaces, where there's a risk of being seen. This kink plays on the thrill of exhibitionism and the danger of discovery, often featured in erotica to escalate the stakes and excitement of an encounter.

Exhibition: Different from public play, this involves performing sexual acts for an audience, often in a controlled or safe environment. It explores the desire to display and share one's sexuality with others, touching on themes of voyeurism, exhibitionism, and performance.

Chastity Play: Involves a person being required to wear a chastity device to prevent sexual release, often controlled by a partner. This practice emphasizes themes of submission, control, and delayed gratification, adding a layer of psychological play to physical desire.

Sensory Play: The use of various stimuli (such as feathers, ice, or scented oils) to arouse the senses during sexual activity. Sensory play in erotica can enhance the immersive experience for the reader, focusing on the detailed exploration of touch, taste, smell, sight, and sound.

Leather Fetish: Involves a specific attraction to leather garments or accessories, often within the context of BDSM.

Leather fetish scenes in erotica highlight the sensory experiences associated with leather and its cultural significance within the BDSM community.

Dominatrix: A woman who takes the dominant role in BDSM activities. She controls the scene, dictating the actions and responses of the submissive partner. Dominatrix-led scenarios in erotica explore themes of female empowerment, dominance, and the intricate dance of power exchange, often challenging traditional gender roles and expectations.

Switch: A person who enjoys and is capable of playing both the dominant and submissive roles in BDSM interactions. The fluidity of a switch's preferences allows for a dynamic exploration of power dynamics in erotica, highlighting the versatility and complexity of human sexual expression.

Financial Domination: A BDSM practice where the submissive derives pleasure from giving money or gifts to the dominant. This niche yet increasingly popular theme in erotica delves into power dynamics, control, and the psychological aspects of submission and dominance extended into the financial realm.

Ménage à Trois: A sexual arrangement involving three people. While commonly associated with polyamory or threesomes, in erotica, it specifically refers to scenes where all three participants are involved sexually, offering a narrative space to explore complex interpersonal dynamics and heightened erotic tension.

Queening: A sexual practice where a woman sits on her partner's face, allowing for oral-genital or oral-anal stimulation. This act of dominance and submission can be a powerful display of female sexuality and empowerment in erotica, emphasizing the pleasure and control dynamics between partners.

Shibari: The art of Japanese rope bondage, characterized by intricate patterns and knots. Shibari scenes in erotica not only focus on the aesthetic and sensual aspects of bondage but also delve into the deep trust and communication required between partners, making it a rich theme for exploring complex emotional and physical connections.

CNC (Consensual Non-Consent): A BDSM practice where participants agree to act out scenarios that simulate non-consensual sex within a safe, controlled, and consensual environment. CNC themes in erotica can be challenging and provocative, requiring careful navigation to maintain the boundaries of consent and fantasy.

Sapiosexual: A term describing individuals who find intelligence to be the most sexually attractive feature in a partner. Erotica that includes sapiosexual characters often focuses on intellectual connection as a primary driver of sexual attraction, adding a layer of mental stimulation to the physical arousal.

Furry Fetish: An interest in anthropomorphic animal characters with human personalities and characteristics, often involving costumes or animated representations. Furry fetish erotica explores themes of identity, fantasy, and alternative expressions of sexuality through the lens of furry culture.

Tantric Sex: An ancient practice that emphasizes sexual activities as a form of spiritual and physical connection, focusing on prolonged and mindful experiences rather than immediate gratification. Erotica incorporating tantric sex often delves into themes of emotional depth, intimacy, and the exploration of sexual energy as a transformative force.

Lactation: Refers to arousal and sexual pleasure derived from breastfeeding or lactation. This niche interest within erotica explores themes of nurturing, intimacy, and the eroticization of bodily functions, offering a deep dive into the psychology of desire and taboo.

Puppy Play: A form of role-play within BDSM where participants adopt the roles of puppies and their caretakers. This practice emphasizes the dynamics of care, discipline, and the innocence associated with puppy behavior, exploring non-human role-play within a consensual BDSM context.

Sounding: Involves the insertion of rods into the urethra for sexual stimulation. This advanced and somewhat niche practice within erotica challenges conventional boundaries of pleasure and pain, focusing on the exploration of body limits and sensations.

Latex Fetish: A fascination or sexual arousal stemming from the look, feel, or smell of latex worn on the body. Erotica incorporating latex fetish delves into sensory experiences, highlighting the material's unique properties as a means of enhancing sexual encounters.

Breath Control Play: A BDSM activity that involves controlling a partner's breathing during sexual play. This practice, while risky, introduces themes of trust, surrender, and the manipulation of bodily responses for heightened arousal in erotica narratives.

Wax Play: Involves dripping hot wax onto the skin for pleasure and pain. This form of temperature play in erotica explores the fine line between discomfort and arousal, using sensory contrast to heighten the erotic experience.

Cuckquean: The female counterpart to a cuckolding scenario, where a woman derives pleasure from watching her partner engage sexually with someone else. This term reflects the exploration of jealousy, voyeurism, and sexual liberation from a female perspective within erotica.

Foot Fetish: A sexual interest focused on feet, where arousal is derived from the visual, tactile, or olfactory aspects of feet. Erotica that explores foot fetishism can delve into the specifics of this fascination, offering narratives that celebrate this particular form of body worship.

Gangbang: Refers to sexual scenarios involving one individual having sex with multiple partners in succession or at the same time. This term in erotica often explores themes of surrender, endurance, and the dynamics of group sexual activities.

Knife Play: A form of risk-aware consensual kink involving the use of knives for sexual gratification. This practice within erotica explores the thrill of danger, the aesthetics of sharpness, and trust between partners, emphasizing the psychological aspects of playing with fear and control.

Humiliation Play: A BDSM activity that involves consensual psychological humiliation for arousal. Erotica incorporating this theme investigates the power of words and actions to evoke shame, submission, and pleasure, offering a complex look at emotional and psychological dynamics.

Spanking: A common practice within BDSM and general erotica that involves striking the buttocks to induce pain and pleasure. This activity emphasizes the balance between domination and submission, often serving as a form of foreplay or punishment within erotic narratives.

Flogging: A form of impact play that involves using a whip or floss to strike the body, typically focusing on the back or buttocks. Flogging can range from gentle to severe, introducing elements of pain, control, and trust into erotica stories.

Corsetry: The use of corsets for aesthetic, erotic, or restrictive purposes. In erotica, corsetry may symbolize constriction and control, enhancing the physical form while also playing into themes of historical fetishism and body modification.

Sensual Massage: A practice that involves the use of touch and massage techniques to arouse and stimulate a partner. This term in erotica often highlights the importance of intimacy, connection, and the exploration of pleasure through tactile sensations.

Nipple Play: Refers to the stimulation of nipples through licking, biting, sucking, or the use of toys for sexual pleasure. This form of erotic engagement is common in erotica, exploring the sensitivity and erotic potential of this erogenous zone.

Sex Toy Use: The incorporation of sex toys, such as vibrators, dildos, or anal beads, into sexual activities. Erotica that features sex toy use often delves into themes of exploration, pleasure enhancement, and the breaking down of sexual inhibitions.

Body Worship: A practice that involves intense adoration and erotic focus on a partner's body parts. In erotica, body worship can serve as a form of devotion and submission, highlighting the beauty and sensuality of the human form.

Erotic Dance: The use of dance movements to seduce or arouse a partner or audience. This term in erotica captures the allure and power of movement, rhythm, and physical expression as tools of seduction and erotic storytelling.

Caging: A BDSM practice where the submissive is confined in a cage as part of a scene or for an extended period. This practice explores themes of control, surrender, and confinement, adding a dimension of power dynamics to erotica narratives.

Pony Play: A subset of animal role-play where participants adopt the roles and behaviors of ponies, often involving costumes, training, and showmanship. This unique form of role-play explores themes of domination, training, and exhibitionism within a consensual, fantasy-based context.

Watersports: A term that refers to sexual activities involving urine, such as urination on or by a sexual partner. While considered a niche kink, watersports in erotica explore the boundaries of taboo and the eroticization of acts that defy conventional sexual norms.

Electrostimulation: The use of electrical impulses to stimulate the nerves for sexual pleasure. This practice introduces a technological aspect to erotica, exploring the intersections between human sensation, pleasure, and electronic devices.

Teabagging: A colloquial term referring to the act of placing one's testicles in the mouth of a partner. In erotica, teabagging can be used to explore themes of sexual playfulness, oral pleasure, and the erotic potential of less commonly depicted sexual acts.

Afterword

Writing erotica that flies off the shelves isn't just about steamy scenes; it's about connecting with your readers. Think about what makes a story irresistible to you. Is it the characters, the tension, or how the story makes you feel? Use that insight to fuel your writing. Remember, the best stories come from a place of authenticity—write what excites you, and chances are, it'll excite your readers, too.

Finding your unique voice can seem daunting, but it's simpler than you might think. Start by writing the way you talk. This helps keep your stories genuine and relatable. Your readers are looking for an escape, and your natural voice is the perfect guide. Don't worry about sounding like anyone else; your distinct style is what will make your readers come back for more.

Don't shy away from exploring different themes and kinks. Erotica is a wide-open space where you can experiment with various scenarios and dynamics. This attention to detail enriches your story and builds trust with your readers.

Promoting your book might seem like a hurdle, but there are simple, effective ways to get noticed. Social media is an excellent tool for connecting directly with your audience. Share snippets of your work **subtly**, engage in conversations and let your personality shine through. Readers love getting to know the person behind the words. **Don't get BANNED! Don't PROMOTE! ENGAGE!**

Another great way to promote your work is through erotica-focused & promoted newsletters. These platforms cater to readers already interested in your genre, making them an ideal audience for your book. Look into submission guidelines and reach out—you might find a new group of readers eager for your stories. **Tip: Free, then 99-cent promos work best in promotional newsletters. Not often do you see a newsletter allowing a 2.99 or regular-priced book. Something to think about: if they do, you won't make your money back unless it's Bookbub. Just my thoughts!**

Networking with other erotica authors can also open doors you didn't know existed. Join online forums, attend workshops, and participate in writing groups. These communities offer support, advice, and opportunities for collaboration. Plus, it's always encouraging to connect with people who understand the unique challenges and joys of writing erotica.

Remember, writing is a journey with ups and downs. There will be days when the words flow effortlessly, and others when writing a single sentence is a struggle. That's perfectly normal. The key is to keep going, exploring, and refining your craft. Every word you write brings you closer to mastering the art of erotica.

Don't forget the power of a captivating cover and a tantalizing book description. These are the first things a potential reader sees, so make them irresistible. A professional cover that hints at the steaminess inside and a description that teases the reader's imagination can make all the difference in attracting attention.

Engage with your readers wherever you can. Whether through email newsletters, blog posts, or social media, building a relationship with your audience is invaluable. Listen to their feedback, answer their questions, and tell them you appreciate their support. A loyal reader is a treasure worth more than gold.

Lastly, never underestimate the importance of editing. A well-edited book reads better and shows your readers you value their time reading and money. Whether fixing typos, tightening up scenes, or ensuring the plot flows smoothly, taking the time to polish your work pays off in the end.

Writing bestselling erotica isn't about following a secret formula; it's about passion, perseverance, and connecting with your readers. Keep exploring, keep writing, and remember—every author was once a beginner. Believe in your stories, and don't be afraid to share them with the world. Your next book could be the one that captures hearts and ignites imaginations. Keep writing, and let your passion lead the way.